ECHO

ECHO
NEW EDEN BOOK 4

JESSICA MARTING

SHADOW PRESS

Echo (New Eden Book 4)

ISBN 978-1-989780-40-4

Copyright © 2025 by J.L. Turner

Edited by Autumn Reed

Cover design by German Creative

Content notes: Death of a partner; discussion of a natural disaster and mass casualty event; pregnancy.

For David, again.

The human was here. His sensors had improved while he regenerated, sharpening the connection with his implanted hardware and his new body's organic systems. The human had been visiting him since his enhanced brain could recognize noises, speaking to him in a language he didn't fully understand, the tones and cadences foreign to a being that was more machine than flesh. He was unsure how much time had passed since he'd gained the first shred of sentience, only that the human had been nearby almost constantly.

He could discern now that the human was likely female. Her footsteps were lighter than he expected his would be, should he ever have to walk, something he had never tried but instinctively knew how to do. Her voice, faraway as it sounded, pitched between 178 and 182 hertz, punctuated by what he could now identify as weeping. An excessively emotional reaction, one he did not have the hardware or personal experience to parse through and examine. But in his moments of clarity that were occurring more frequently, he found he didn't mind her presence. He noticed her absence when she wasn't there.

He was floating in something and could not speak. His system report informed him that he had developed vocal cords, that his cerebrum was fully formed, but words would not come. His understanding of the language she spoke slowly grew, as if his programming was feeding him words one at a time. He could now recognize her words, even if he didn't grasp their meaning.

"I love you. Come back to me."

———

A BUMP to the head woke Pauline. She started, ready to curse out whoever had smacked her, then belatedly realized she'd done it to herself. Her head had collided with the giant tank she had been spending almost all her waking hours beside. And sleeping hours, she thought ruefully, rubbing the sore spot on her head. She'd dozed off beside the tank again. Beside Aiden, who floated in it, waiting to be woken up.

No, he was waiting to be *activated*. She could practically hear Connor, New Eden's resident medic, firmly reminding her of the correct cyborg terminology. Aiden was going to be activated any day now. And he wasn't Aiden—he had died in an electrical accident weeks ago. This was AL17, the seventeenth clone of a man who, hundreds of years ago, signed up for a top-secret black ops military experiment.

Pauline gazed at the tank. AL17's limbs gently bobbed in the water. Wires and cables snaked from ports throughout his body, and metal pieces embedded in his skin faintly glowed in the dim light offered by the cloning room, an extension of the cyborgs' starship's sickbay. It had been Pauline's home for weeks as she waited for AL17's cloning to complete.

The floor around the tank was surrounded by cards and letters she had written, punctuated by the occasional bouquet of dandelions, crispy with age. Rising, she stretched her back and yawned. "Good morning," she said to the unconscious clone. She pressed her free hand to the tank. So close to him, yet so far.

AL17 didn't move.

"I fell asleep again," Pauline said sheepishly. Injecting as much levity into her voice as she could, she continued. "It'll be a lot easier when you're awake and we can go home again. I've put off moving out of my old house until you can come back. I figured it would be more familiar to you in the early days. Plus, when we're ready to move into our new house, I thought you'd want some input. It'll be a lot of work, but I think we can create a beautiful home together. Rhys and Hannah just moved into theirs two days ago. Remember Rhys? RH103, I think his designation used to be?" Tears clogged her throat, but she kept speaking, hoping he could hear her somehow.

Jealousy, hot and ugly, twisted in Pauline's belly when she thought about the other couple. Hannah had everything Pauline used to have—a cyborg partner who adored her, who had survived his own horrifying medical ordeal, and now a new home to share.

"Anyway, we'll get there again," Pauline said when she recovered her voice. "We have to get to know each other again, but that was fun the first time, wasn't it?" An unexpected wave of heat stirred at the memory of their first meeting, when the cyborgs' starship broke New Eden's atmosphere in the middle of the night. Their connection had been instant and electric, love and lust at first sight. She could only hope it would happen again for them. The tears she had been suppressing returned, sliding down her cheeks. "I miss you," she said softly.

AL17 floated in the water, unmoving. His eyelids remained closed, fringed by dark lashes that had grown in a few days ago. Aiden's skin had been tan, made deeper by the near-relentless glow offered by New Eden's twin suns, but in the tank, he looked sort of faded without it. It was the same with his dark hair, which had only recently started to grow. His new body was still muscular, although not as huge as he'd been the first time they met. He'd once told her that he'd had plenty of time to exercise in their destroyed terraformed asteroid and later on their starship. Even floating in a tank, AL17 was still the most attractive man Pauline had ever seen.

"Good bye, love," she said, blowing him a kiss. "I should probably get some real sleep at home, maybe a bite to eat. I'll be back soon."

She left the sickbay, knowing the route to the ship's exterior airlock by heart. Her footsteps dully echoed off the metal deck, her arms appearing sallow in the overhead illumination, dimmed to conserve fuel. The craft had food processors and replicators on board, but she hadn't dared to use them for fear of breaking something. She hadn't realized she was hungry until she left AL17.

At the airlock, the ship's exterior door opened before she could pull on it. Connor stepped inside, his dark eyebrows lifting in surprise when he saw her. "Have you been here all night?" he asked by way of greeting.

"Is it morning? I've lost track of time." The space between her shoulder blades ached, a sure sign that she had spent the night aboard. Most of the ship was devoid of windows, at least the areas Pauline had access to, and the cyborgs didn't seem to embrace clocks.

"It is half past six in the morning," Connor replied. "I've come by to check on our favorite patient."

"He seems to be the same," Pauline replied.

"He is improving every morning. His body is fully formed by now." Connor strode through the ship's corridors. Her exhaustion and hunger forgotten, she followed him back to the sickbay.

Connor activated the rest of the lights before examining AL17. Pauline blinked, her eyes watering. He slowly walked around the tank, a critical look in his metallic eyes. Periodically, he checked the readouts on the monitors hooked up to the tank.

His silence was unnerving. "Is he okay?" she asked.

Connor nodded. "Yes. I may be able transfer him to a regular bed today."

Hope flared in Pauline's heart for the first time in weeks. "Really? You'll wake Aiden today?"

"No," Connor said sharply. "We will be *activating* AL17."

Pauline bristled at the response. He had told her multiple times that Aiden had died and the new clone wouldn't be him, but she couldn't bring herself to believe that. The other cyborgs had memories of the men they'd been cloned from—their originals—and those of their previous iterations. It stood to reason that AL17 could remember being Aiden and would remember Pauline. "Of course," she muttered, tamping down her irritation at Connor's tone. "Can I be there when he's activated?"

Connor hesitated before replying. "I'm not certain that's a good idea."

Indignation, then anger had her straightening her spine. "Is there any reason I shouldn't be?"

"Only if you continue to refuse to acknowledge that this man is not Aiden."

It took everything Pauline had to keep from shrieking at Connor. When she replied, her voice was level. "Of course. I just thought he would probably remember me and wanted to be a friendly face, you know?"

Connor waited before replying again. When he did, his response was gentler than usual, as if he could sense her frustration. "Memories are not always transferred to new clones. He will be aware of the connection he has with his fellow cyborgs, even if he can't remember us. He has been programmed with our collective knowledge of what we are. I cannot do anything else to his memory banks. If you are present when he is activated, you must remain calm when he awakens. Do not startle him or show excessive emotion. It is imperative that he activates in a neutral environment." A line worried between his brows. "Perhaps it would be best if you refrained from attending the activation altogether."

"I'll be good!" she promised. "I won't cry, no matter what, I promise." She dearly hoped she could keep that promise.

"I will hold you to that," Connor said. Pauline knew he would. Glancing at the tank, his eyes widened. "Look at that. His hand."

Pauline's gaze landed on AL17's hand. His fingers twitched, then flexed. The movement was too great to be that of someone in stasis. "Oh, my God!" she squealed.

"He definitely will be transferred today," Connor announced.

Pauline scrubbed her leaking eyes with the hem of her shirt.

Aiden would be back with her soon.

CHAPTER TWO

IT WAS COLD.

This was the first time his body had ever registered a change in external temperature. His system took two nanoseconds to register the shift before adjusting his core temperature to compensate. He relaxed, the goose bumps on his skin reverting as quickly as they'd appeared, although he noted he was outside the warm cocoon of the tank he'd previously spent his entire existence in. The change aroused mild curiosity in him, as did the realization that he was moving. Or rather, something was under him and it was moving him forward. Could he move himself? He experimentally wiggled an appendage—his right foot, according to his brain's readout.

Don't get up yet. Not until you're finished downloading your memory program. The voice popped into his head, clear and authoritative.

Who are you? he asked.

My cyborg designation is CW44, but you can call me Connor.

Am I a cyborg? he asked. He didn't remember until now that he didn't know what he was, just that he existed.

Yes. Your designation is AL17. You are the seventeenth cloned iteration of a human man whose designation was AL.

Fascinating. Am I a cloned human, then? Have I been created with the DNA of other species?

No. You are a cybernetically enhanced human male. Your physical strength and emotional intelligence will improve in the coming days, after you are activated.

He found himself looking forward to such an event. *When can I look forward to activation?*

Within the next twenty-four hours, after your memory uploads are complete.

Another dozen questions popped into his mind, all of which clamored to be answered first. *What is this state called?*

Regeneration.

What happened to the clone designated AL16?

CW44 hesitated before replying. *It is best to talk about that at a later time.*

How long have I been in this regenerative state?

Sixteen weeks, by the calendar of the planet we live on.

Where am I?

New Eden, a minor planet in the 4-Jericho-7 Sector. There is little else nearby.

Who is the other person who spoke to me?

CW44 didn't reply. He thought their connection might have been lost. An odd ache spread through him at the loss, a feeling he didn't have a word for. A few seconds later, CW44 spoke. *She was a companion to AL16.*

She was female, as he had suspected. *What is her designation? When can I speak to her? Can she speak to me, as you are now?*

No. This is a conversation for another time. The movement abruptly stopped. *It is time to rest again for the upload.*

———

PAULINE HAD SUMMONED the mental fortitude necessary to clean her house from top to bottom, spurred on by the knowledge that Aiden was returning to her soon and her need to make a positive impression on him. She had always been a bit of a slob, inheriting messy habits from her father, who had died eight years prior. Her heart squeezed when she thought of him. He would have approved of Aiden, she was sure.

Shaking off her melancholy, she boiled some eggs for a meal, remembering that New Eden would soon have regular meat stores again for the first time since the quake. Led by Hannah, the agri-center was now raising cattle, and the cyborgs had devised a way to clone meat, at least until the cows were old enough to slaughter. A shudder of revulsion coursed through Pauline when she thought of that, since the calves were so cute, making her grateful that she didn't work in food production.

Aiden had expressed interest in trying steak. Maybe they could learn how to prepare steaks together.

There was so much they could do together. Her body flooded with forgotten heat from her memories. Their initial attraction had been instant, the most powerful emotion she'd ever felt. She had every reason to believe she and AL17 could have that again.

Pauline had just finished eating a tomato salad, generously garnished with fresh herbs from the agri-center, when a knock sounded at her front door. Setting aside the bowl, she quickly answered it. Jasmine and Simon, one of Jasmine's cyborg partners, stood on the other side. Both of them wore pensive looks on their faces, as if they were nervous about what they had to say. Pauline's stomach dropped. "What happened?" she asked. The tomatoes she'd just eaten threatened to reappear.

"AL17 is ready to be activated," Simon said. There was

a serious note in his voice, no trace of a smile to be found on his face.

Despite the gravity in his demeanor, Pauline's heart leaped. "Really? Oh my God, let's go!" She stepped out of the house, forgetting that she wasn't wearing shoes until her soles touched the gray wooden stoop.

"Pauline, wait for a minute," Jasmine said. Her usual cheerful expression was gone, replaced by one that matched Simon's serious mien. "It's really important that you understand that *AL17* is being activated." She shot a quick, nervous glance at Simon, whose lips thinned in response.

"Yeah, I know." Another iteration of AL16, of Aiden. Not the exact same man, but very close.

"The next part of his life is learning how to be a person again," Simon continued. "That can take a few weeks or more. And you have to understand that we haven't done this in about twenty-five years, so we're rusty, and the cloning techniques used for him are a little different."

Pauline nodded. "I know." The Si'laar—the water-dwelling species they now shared the planet with—had offered help via upgraded equipment when Aiden was cloned.

"*And* we've never done this with people from outside our society. We're all kind of flying blind here," Simon added.

"Connor said as much." Pauline slid into her sandals. "I'm ready to go to the sickbay."

"Pauline!" Jasmine's voice was unusually sharp. Simon started at her tone. When she spoke again, her voice was softer. "Look, we don't want to see you more hurt and grieving than you already are. If you're going to be there when he wakes up, you have to understand that he isn't Aiden."

Pauline stilled. A curious mix of white-hot rage and frustration welled in her, the near-constant repetition of a variation on that phrase from everyone—Connor, Rhys, Hannah, and now Jasmine and Simon—making her want to scream. She wasn't an idiot; she knew that already. Tamping down her emotions, she pasted what she hoped was a friendly smile on her face. "I understand. I still want to be there when he wakes up. Hopefully, he'll remember the connection we had."

"Pauline…" Jasmine's voice was gentle, tinged with sadness.

Shit, she shouldn't have said that. "Maybe he'll still have some of Aiden's memories," she hastily added. "Didn't you remember Darius when you were last cloned, Simon?" She'd heard that story before. Simon and Darius had a history before they arrived on New Eden, before they met Jasmine, although she wasn't privy to all the details.

A blush crept up Simon's neck. "That was different. We had both recently been activated, we're both cybernetically enhanced. You…"

"And I'm none of those things," Pauline finished for him. Simon gave her the barest of nods.

She reminded herself they were trying to help, to insulate her heart against further pain. She wanted to tell them that they knew nothing of the instant attraction she and Aiden had shared. The cyborgs had innate traits and instincts that were part of who they were, before the cybernetic components were embedded and programmed into them. Aiden, not the machine, had loved her. It was perfectly reasonable to assume that AL17 would have the same feelings for her, eventually.

She didn't say that to Jasmine and Simon, not wanting to provoke an argument. Not when she was so close to meeting Aiden again. "I'm glad you're looking out for me," she said. "I mean it. But I need you to understand that I'm an adult. I can handle whatever comes at me when AL17 and I see each other again."

"Meet," Jasmine corrected her. "You'll be *meeting* AL17 for the first time today."

"And he may not be amenable to speaking with his physical voice," Simon cautioned.

"I thought you had all stopped using your cyborg telepathy link," Pauline said.

"AL17 will probably be using it with the rest of us. It goes with being cloned." Worry formed a line between Simon's brows. "Are you certain you want to come to the sickbay for this? It might be best to wait a day or two until AL17 has more of his bearings, so to speak."

Pauline shook her head. "No. And I'm tired of arguing over this. Let's go." Closing the door behind her, she walked away. A few seconds later, Jasmine and Simon joined her.

———

IT IS *time for you to activate.* The cyborg designated as CW44 didn't make a suggestion so much as a command.

How do I do that? AL17 asked. His programming was complete. He felt as if he had the weight of the knowledge of the known universe crammed into his head. He had no idea where to start with the sum of it, to parse out which pieces he would need to survive.

I am going to disconnect you from the starship's mainframe. As I do so, your physical body will be able to rise, and your organic systems will be fully integrated with your cybernetic self. CW44 sounded a little sheepish. *You will have to forgive me should something go awry. I have never activated a fellow cyborg in my current iteration, and you were cloned using some new methods I haven't worked with before. I thought it best that you activate in the open instead of the tank. It was easier for me to monitor your lung function this way.*

AL17's chest heaved. He realized he was breathing. *My respiratory function is online.*

Yes, I think everything is as it should be. I have finished disconnecting you. You will activate naturally and wake up when your body is ready. We will meet soon.

A strange sensation coursed through AL17. A chill swept along his veins, and he realized he had been disconnected from something he hadn't known he was a part of until now. The starship, perhaps? An image of a black shape hurtling through stars filled his mind. Was that the ship he was aboard, or was it merely a reference file implanted in his mind?

He reached out to CW44. *Is she here?*

No answer.

CW44? Are you still here? Is she here too? His questions went unanswered.

Am I alone? Where did you go? CW44?

His physical body jerked. His lower half twisted. *Pain,* his brain's processor reported. He was in pain.

His eyes popped open of their own accord. *I have eyes!* His gaze fixed on something above him, white-colored and dotted with lights. A ceiling?

"Aiden?"

She was here. He tried to turn his head in the direction of her voice. Tried, and failed as his body struggled to come back online.

Who is Aiden?

CHAPTER THREE

Pauline's breath caught at the sight of the man lying in a bed before her. His dark hair was close-cropped to his head, far shorter than what Aiden had sported. He was paler too, but that would change once he spent some time in the sun. He was nude, save for a towel placed over his hips.

"This is the first time in our history that we have activated one of our own outside the tank," Connor said, then launched into a history of cloning practices. They'd recently learned that much of their cloning tech had been stolen from the Si'laar years ago by their previous iterations. The Si'laar had made recent improvements and passed them on to the cyborgs.

Pauline nodded along politely, her calm demeanor a mask for the trepidation and excitement that welled in her.

There was an audience for the activation that she hadn't been expecting. Simon was assisting Connor, monitoring Aiden's vital signs on clearscreens around the room. Jasmine and Darius waited nearby, worried looks on their faces. Rhys and Hannah were there too.

Pauline pushed away all thoughts of the others surrounding her, focusing on Aiden and Connor, the only people she'd expected to be here today. Connor removed a wire plugged into one of Aiden's wrist ports and held his fingers over it, his lips thinned in concentration. Aiden's fingers twitched, then his legs jumped, as if he'd been sparked by electricity.

Pauline closed her eyes for a few seconds, remembering how he'd died. *Bad analogy.*

Aiden took a few deep, wheezing breaths, the first major sign of life he'd shown so far. Pauline leaned forward, reaching for one of his hands, only for Connor to push her away. "Not now," he murmured. She took a half step back, feeling as if she'd been burned.

A few moments passed in silence, all eyes on the cyborg before them as his breathing picked up a normal rhythm, his chest rising and falling. His eyelids twitched, but his eyes didn't open. "AL17's systems are online and functioning optimally," Connor finally reported. Rhys nodded. Pauline spotted Jasmine and Simon reaching for each other's hands, as if they were the ones who needed support right now.

Stop thinking like that, she admonished herself. Simon had lost a lifelong friend when Aiden died, all the cyborgs had. Simon was grieving too.

Aiden took a deep, shuddering breath, then opened his eyes. Pauline's heart leaped. "Aiden?" she breathed, voice barely a whisper.

He turned his head to face her, his expression blank. His eyes were different—a lighter color, or maybe it was because of the metal components in them. There was no flicker of recognition on his face, but that had to come later, didn't it?

Didn't it?

Aiden turned his head back to its original position, gaze fixed on the ceiling. "My designation is AL17," he said. His voice was devoid of emotion. Turning his head away from Pauline, he said, "You are the cybernetic human designated CW44, are you not?"

Connor nodded. "Yes, but I am called Connor."

"You are the one designated RH103," Aiden said to Rhys.

"Yes." Rhys didn't bother to correct Aiden on his name.

"And SP29," Aiden continued.

Simon nodded. "And one of my partners, Jasmine."

Curiosity flickered over Aiden's face so quickly that Pauline would have missed it if she hadn't been watching his expression so closely. Maybe he remembered the concept of romantic partners? She took a half step forward. "Aiden, it's me," she said. "Pauline."

His gaze swiveled back to her, studying her intently. "My designation is AL17," he replied. His voice lacked emotion or signs of recognition. It was Aiden's voice, yet it wasn't.

Something in Pauline twisted and broke. She tried to speak, but her voice failed her as a lump filled her throat. When she found her voice, all she could get out was a croaked, "You picked another name before. I helped. We—"

"Pauline," said Connor quietly.

She ignored him. "I'm Pauline. We shared a house before, remember? We love each other." A fresh wave of tears filled her eyes. Goddamn it, she was tired of crying, and she had promised not to during Aiden's activation.

Aiden sat up, swinging his legs over the side of the bed. "I require additional recharging," he announced, heedless of Pauline's heart breaking again. His modesty covering fell away when he got off the bed and walked through the sickbay, presumably to the recharging pods once used by the cyborgs, without a backward glance.

The sickbay was silent. Pauline was afraid that if she spoke first, she might start screaming.

"I'm sorry," Jasmine finally said. She clumsily reached for Pauline, holding her in a loose hug that Pauline didn't reciprocate. It took everything in her not to push her away, but she needed the contact, for fear she would collapse to the deck.

"I tried to tell her," Connor began, then shut his mouth when Rhys and Simon gave him sharp glances.

Pauline's voice shook when she found it. "You did, a lot." She thought about the flowers she'd left at the tank, the letters she'd written on paper brought back from the nearest waystation. Aiden had written her letters before he died, goofy rhymes about how much he loved her, that he left around the house for her to find. To Rhys and Simon, she said, "Don't get mad at him. He's a good medic. He tried to prepare me for this, and I didn't listen." She tried and failed to paste a smile on her face. "Thank you for cloning him. I'm sure he'll appreciate it once he realizes he's alive again." *Damn it!* She corrected herself. "Alive. Just alive."

The man who had just strode away from the sickbay wasn't Aiden. The man she'd carried a vigil for was gone, dead and buried in the cemetery in the western part of the settlement, his DNA twisted apart, refined, and fed into a machine to produce a new, different person.

He's really gone.

A fresh wave of grief crashed into her with such force that she took an involuntary step back. Simon moved with an inhuman speed to grasp her elbow before she could fall over. Shaking him off, she muttered, "I'm fine." Jasmine caught her eye, and she knew that she didn't believe Pauline. "I'm not, but I will be someday."

The sickbay suddenly felt too small, airless. She needed to get out. "Excuse me." Without another word, she bolted out of the sickbay, through the ship's corridors, and out of the airlock, taking in greedy gulps of air as soon as she was out.

———

AL17 INSTINCTIVELY KNEW where the recharging pods were. He made a beeline for them, his bare feet slapping against a metal deck that his sensors reported was supposed to be cold. Funny how he could feel the chill on his bare skin, but it didn't bother him as he suspected it should. He had the vague notion that unenhanced humans were sensitive to temperature extremes.

He realized after he found the corridor lined with pods that he was being guided by the starship, that he was a part of the ship. Its blueprints and schematics easily filled his head when he thought about them, along with detailed dossiers of every cyborg who made up the crew, twenty in all. They had the same style of letter and number designations as he did, but all had other names too. He noted that AL16 was listed as well, the name Aiden Lewis appended on the dossier. AL16 had been a pilot, his previous iterations having combat experience, and he was listed as deceased, the date of death occurring sixteen weeks ago. He was the only recent death among the cyborg brethren.

Something stirred in him at the revelation. Sadness, maybe? Grief for a previous iteration? Was that possible for someone who was mostly machine?

He accessed a file labeled ACTIVATION_PROCE-DURES and downloaded it, data streaming across his vision. According to it, he was supposed to recharge in the pods—an instinct he'd already followed—but there were supposed to be other cyborgs aboard the ship too. Why was he alone? According to the file, he had everything he physically needed to be alive. Yet the social aspect was missing. There were supposed to be other cyborgs here for that purpose.

He supposed that, if he was better socialized, he might be put out about this development. He might feel hurt at being forgotten by all of his cyborg brethren, other than RH103, SP29, and CW44. But he wasn't, so he stepped into a pod and connected himself to the ship.

You need clothing. The reminder came out of nowhere, as did the explanation that sufficient clothing could be found in hard goods lockers in the belly of the ship. Clothing oneself was good manners in cybernetic and New Eden societies.

He reached out to the broadcast link he knew was shared among all the cyborgs, the way CW44 had connected with him before he'd been activated. *Is anyone aboard?*

His only reply was silence. Perhaps he hadn't reached out correctly. *Hello? I'm aboard this ship, and I believe I may be alone.*

No one replied.

Was the sad, crying blonde woman connected to the network? She seemed to care a great deal about him for some reason and would answer if he called. *Pauline? Are you there?*

She didn't reply. She must be entirely organic, he decided.

His cybernetics alerted him to a pending automatic

shutdown for recharging. He leaned back in the pod and closed his eyes, waiting for his systems to automatically send him to sleep. As he drifted off, the image of Pauline came to mind, her sad, beautiful face a curiosity to be explored.

CHAPTER FOUR

How THE FUCK could her house feel even emptier than before? Pauline scrubbed away angry tears with the hem of her tunic, stifling a sob, even though no one could hear her.

She'd been an idiot. An optimistic idiot who hadn't listened to the person who was a literal expert in cloning. If she had just fucking listened to him in the first place, she wouldn't feel like her heart was being put through a thresher again. She might have given herself the opportunity to grieve, to heal.

It took every shred of discipline she had to keep from opening her mouth and screaming, knowing it would draw anyone nearby to her house, and she'd be forced to talk to them. As it was, a knock at the door made her want to do that, anyway. Pinching the bridge of her nose between her fingers, she muttered, "That better not be someone trying to cheer me up."

She stalked back to the front door and swung it open. Relief poured through her when she saw who was on the other side—James Thierry, recently returned from wandering around the uninhabited north for the last five years. "Thank God," she said.

"Hey." His ginger eyebrows were drawn together in concern. Beneath them, his organic eye had a look of concern reflected in it. His cybernetic eye shone in the light of the twin suns overhead.

"You're not here to cheer me up, are you?" she asked.

"Of course not. I'd never try to do that. Can I come in?"

"Yeah." She stepped aside for him. "Did Connor tell you what happened?" They were partners, newly living together. Connor often cloned seafood found in the north for James, using the starship's equipment.

"Of course. He thought I'd be the least worst person to send to see how you're doing." His expression softened. "I'm so sorry, Pauline."

James was the only person on New Eden who let her be angry about Aiden's death. In turn, she hadn't encouraged him to rejoin New Eden society like nothing had happened; she hadn't expected him to pick up and pretend to be the person he was before he exiled himself for years. While they hadn't been particularly close before he left, they had formed a friendship since his return.

A fresh wave of tears filled her eyes at James's condolence. "I wish I'd listened to Connor. That might make things easier."

"You realize that he isn't gloating right now, don't you? He's devastated about this too, even though he isn't that great at showing emotion."

"Except to you," she said wryly. She suspected James and Connor might be more than friends, but she didn't pry.

"That took some time. He said he really does wish he could have explained this better to you in a way you'd understand."

Pauline let out a watery sigh. "He did. I didn't fucking listen." She looked back at the kitchen. "Want some wine? I have a bottle around here somewhere." She'd been saving it for Aiden's arrival, but it was unlikely she'd ever need it for that purpose.

A faint shudder rippled through James. "Ugh, no thank you. Too sour. Don't stop yourself on my account, though."

Pauline didn't want to drink alone. "In that case, I'm good."

"You needed something to look forward to," James said. "You've lost a lot the last few years. You finally had something good to hold on to, and then it was gone." His voice warbled a little on the last couple of words.

"It feels like he died again." She pressed her palms against her eyes in a vain attempt to keep from crying again. "I'm such an idiot."

"You're not." James's voice was unusually firm. Pauline wished she could believe him.

"Everything felt so miraculous when they arrived," she said. "I thought Aiden being cloned again would just be one more amazing thing they could do, and it turns out it wasn't. There are limits to cybernetic technology that I refused to listen to." She turned away and poured a glass of water from the sink's pump and gulped it down. Remembering her manners, she asked, "Want some?"

"No thanks."

"Did you know Simon and Jasmine were there for AL17's activation? Why were they there?" Frustration welled in her. It was irrational—of course Simon had been friends with Aiden—yet she couldn't help but feel angry at their presence.

"Support, probably. You *do* know that Jasmine considers you a friend?"

Did she? They hadn't spent much time together before the cyborgs' arrival. Jasmine and Hannah were the same age and lifelong friends; Rodelle had been their babysitter once upon a time. The three of them had always been close to the exclusion of others. Pauline, at thirty-two, was a few years older than Jasmine and Hannah and had always kept to herself, even before the quake that devastated New Eden. Living on the opposite side of the settlement than the others, she hadn't been especially close to Rodelle, either, despite being close to the same age.

She hadn't realized she was lonely until she met Aiden the first night their ship landed.

She still remembered locking eyes from across the amphitheater that night. The immediate, electrifying connection before they'd spoken a word to each other. The way he'd headed straight for her as soon as Rhys announced that the cyborgs would be rooming with the locals. How Aiden had known they were meant for each other before he knew her name.

James was waiting for an answer. "Yeah, I guess Jasmine and I are friends." As with Hannah, Pauline privately seethed with jealousy when she thought of Jasmine and her partners that were still alive. She braced herself as she considered her next question, even though she knew James was unlikely to judge her for it. "Do you think everyone will expect me to take up with AL17?"

His eyes widened in alarm. "What? No, of course not." Stumbling over his next words, he said, "He isn't Aiden."

"Would I be a bad person if I wanted to tear out the eyes of anyone who looked at AL17, anyway?" The question flew out of her before she could stop herself.

That look didn't leave James's face. "Well, yeah, but only if you actually tore out someone's eyes. You can't help how you feel, only how you react. And I should point out that the only other single woman in this settlement who's the right age is Lauren Lansing, and she's had a thing going with Tommy for a couple of weeks now, since she started working at the seismology center."

That meant all the unattached women on New Eden in their twenties and thirties had taken up with a cyborg. Aiden had told her that a few of his brethren had casual partners in other parts of the galaxy they'd met on their travels, and a couple of them hoped to eventually bring them to New Eden, when improved planetary infrastructure was in place. Simon and Darius already had something together before they met Jasmine.

So, that leaves me alone again. Pauline didn't voice the thought, not wanting to draw a fresh wave of condolences from James. "Yeah, I guess. Do you know what happens with AL17 next?"

"He has to learn how to be a cyborg, I think. I'm not sure of the exact process. I suppose it's like parents raising a kid, maybe? Connor's not sure how to do that."

That admission had Pauline's attention. "What? He's a fucking medic! He's done this before!"

"His previous iterations did. None of them have activated a cyborg since their last collective cloning. And they've never done this on a planet. It was always on their ship or their old asteroid home." James sounded a little grim. "And they've never done it this way, when everyone has regular names. AL17 might be confused. Connor said he started calling for everyone when he locked himself into the recharging pods."

Pauline's heart unexpectedly went out to AL17. He'd seemed so certain of where he was going when he stalked out of the sickbay, unwilling to listen to anything she had to say.

"Connor went back to him after he called, but he was already sleeping," James added.

"Oh my God." Pauline crossed the short distance to the door and shoved her feet into her homemade sandals.

"Where are you going?"

"Back to the ship. I can't just *leave* him there, alone and confused."

"He isn't alone. Connor's checking on him."

"Checking on him isn't the same as helping him." Pauline nearly added the epithet "dumbass" to that statement, but refrained in time. She didn't have a lot of friends and didn't want to lose what she had by taking out her grief on someone else.

James put his hand on her arm, stilling her. "Pauline."

"You're right, I should bring clothes." She shook him off and dashed for the bedroom, where a stack of Aiden's clean clothes was neatly folded, waiting for him. Her heart ached at the sight, but she brushed it off. "I know he isn't Aiden. I'm not going back to the ship to help Aiden. I'm going back to the ship to make sure AL17 is okay. He's probably confused and scared." Shame swept through her as the realization hit her. Aiden wouldn't have wanted her to run away from his clone. He would probably be embarrassed to know that she had. In a way, she was doing this for Aiden, but she would never tell anyone that.

AL17 wasn't Aiden, but he could still be her friend.

———

I'M HERE. *I apologize for leaving you so abruptly.*

CW44's voice filled AL17's mind. Something in AL17 relaxed. *Thank you for returning.* He couldn't speak or move in the pod, since his cybernetics reported that he required another six minutes for his systems to be fully online, but he felt physically relieved at the company in his head.

Your cloning is something of a novelty at the moment. This is the first time I have overseen this in my current iteration, and it's the first time one of us has been successfully cloned on New Eden.

That is the name of the planet we are docked at, is it not?

Yes, CW44 replied. *We have been here nearly a year, all told. We have not uploaded the story of our flight here, which I apologize for. We were much more diligent doing so before our arrival.*

I have a record of an asteroid habitat.

Yes, we terraformed that and lived there for many years. It was destroyed in an ion storm.

And we resettled on New Eden? AL17 asked.

We responded to a distress call and settled here in exchange for helping to rebuild the New Eden settlement, following a natural disaster three years ago.

And my previous iteration assisted with these efforts?

CW44 hesitated before replying. *Yes.*

Curiosity pulled at AL17. *Did AL16 fail in his efforts?*

No, not at all. Another pause. *AL16 had a relationship with one of the New Edeners, a human woman.*

An unenhanced human?

Yes.

What a fascinating thing to learn. *Is the human still alive?*

CW44's response was delayed, as if he was unsure how AL17 would react. *Yes.*

Did she expire in the same way as AL16? he asked.

No, she wasn't there when he died.

Do we not expire and be cloned again?

Yes, but we don't use those terms in front of unenhanced humans. They're much more sensitive to language. And don't *say that in front of Pauline. She was devastated when AL16 died.*

The image of the sad blonde woman returned. *She was the human female in the sickbay?*

Yes, and the woman AL16 was in a relationship with. "Human female" is not the preferred term here. It's too clinical.

Noted. He nearly asked when he could see her again when he felt the ship's pull on him weaken. His muscles relaxed as he realized he was awake and could leave the recharging pod, could open his eyes.

When he did, the blonde woman stood on the deck before him, the expression in her brown eyes unreadable. His heart skipped a beat.

How strange. His heart should be fully functional.

CHAPTER FIVE

AL17's EYES OPENED, his metallic irises fixing on Pauline's face. Her breath caught, and she nearly dropped the pile of fabric in her hands. He was still naked, connected to the recharging pod with wires and cables. He plucked each one from the ports in his body without his gaze ever leaving her face. "Pauline." Her name was a statement on his lips, devoid of emotion or recognition.

She nodded. "Yeah."

He looked like he wanted to speak further but reconsidered. She held out the clothes. "I thought you might want these."

He looked at the proffered clothing and shook his head. "I require a flight suit."

"No, you don't. You don't really fly that much anymore."

AL17 stepped out of the pod. "I am a fighter pilot."

"That was part of your original programming. You haven't been one for a long time."

"CW44 said you cannot speak to me over our shared link."

She sighed. "No. I'm just a regular human."

"You spoke at my tank while I was generating." Another emotionless statement.

Pauline forgot to breathe again. "You remember that?"

"My memory banks registered your presence to the best of their abilities while I was being actively cloned. My cybernetics functions have greatly improved, and following my time in the recharging pod, are fully online. With their assistance, I recognized your voice."

Pauline was unsure how to respond to that. "Congratulations."

He cocked his head, as if processing her statement. He probably was. "What for?"

"Making it out of the tank alive."

"Why would I not survive the cloning procedure? It has been used for many years by this crew."

"One of the other cyborgs can probably tell you more about that. The species you guys stole that tech from also lives on New Eden. You'll probably meet them later tonight, when they come out of the water." She was babbling. She couldn't help it. Being in the presence of a naked man who bore an uncanny resemblance to her dead lover had that effect on her. There were minute differences in their appearances, but it was still jarring. She thrust out the clothes again. "Please, put these on. I beg you."

"Is this not a natural state?" he asked, clearly confused.

"Yes, that's the problem."

"But my flight suit…"

"I'm sure if you ask Connor, he'll tell you that you'll be fine without it for now."

"She is correct," Connor said from behind her. Pauline jumped, startled. Whirling around, she spotted the other cyborg. "That isn't a requirement for cloning. Your programming is coded to seek out suitable clothing. What

Pauline has provided is sufficient." He glanced at the fabric in Pauline's arms and blanched, as if noticing what she had. "Did that belong to Aiden?"

"There's a distinct lack of men's clothing stores on this planet," she said defensively.

"Perhaps Jasmine can sew something unique for AL17," Connor said, emphasizing the cyborg designation.

"Yeah, *perhaps*. Until then, he needs something to wear, and your flight suits are too hot." That was what Aiden told her, anyway. Rhys had been content to wear one for weeks after the cyborgs landed. Pauline shoved the clothes at AL17. "It's not like whatever she makes won't be exactly what I already have. It's the same, as if he used the replicator on board."

AL17 accepted the bundle, peering at the fabric. He unfolded the blue tunic and loose black trousers, the latter having belonged to Aiden before his arrival on New Eden. Pauline knew Connor would recognize them. "There are undergarments and other suitable clothing in the storage lockers," Connor said.

"I thought I required a flight suit," AL17 said.

Damn it, he was on about the flight suit again?

"You do not require one while the ship is docked. Your cybernetics should be able to monitor your physical functions on their own."

A look of confusion crossed AL17's face. "But my programming includes the use of a flight suit."

"It does, but we know now that we don't strictly need them, especially on a place as amenable to human life as New Eden is. What Pauline has brought you is sufficient, as is the spare clothing in storage."

AL17 didn't look convinced, but he nodded, the clothes still in his hands. "What is my designated task today?"

Aiden had worked wherever he was needed most—

helping to construct pre-fab buildings, assisting with livestock cloning, repairs aboard the ship. Pauline's heart squeezed. He had died during such a repair. "They're looking for help at the seismology center," she said. "A few people are working there."

"Including you," Connor pointed out.

The statement felt like an accusation. "Yeah. I'm less likely to break something in seismology than I would be at the power plant."

"What is a power plant?" AL17 asked.

"It's a facility that provides electricity. New Eden has harnessed nearby waterfalls to provide electricity to the settlement," Connor explained.

"And this is an important job?"

"They're all important on a place like New Eden," Pauline said.

"Why don't you get dressed, and I can send you some files about New Eden and our role here?" Connor suggested. "We have not had an opportunity to upload these details into our ship's banks for future iterations."

A shudder rippled through Pauline at the mention of iterations. What was the cyborgs' plan for themselves if this happened again? They were determined to live like New Edeners; did that mean they wouldn't be cloned again if one died? Would they clone New Edeners? Why the hell hadn't they talked about this as a community? It would have been a topic for a useful meeting in the amphitheater. Aiden had died so quickly, and the rest of the cyborgs sprang into action before anyone else could say something.

AL17 nodded. "That information would be appreciated." He started to walk away, bare feet slapping against the metal deck. Pauline cringed. That had to be cold.

"Where are you going?" she asked.

"To the storage lockers," he replied without turning his

head. "According to my programming and CW44, I require the use of more clothing than this to be considered socially acceptable on this planet."

Pauline didn't move, instead watching him walk away with a quiet confidence she wouldn't have expected from a day-old cyborg. *Goddamn it, he looks just like Aiden from the back.* He'd had such a grabbable ass.

Her face heated and she looked at the deck. When she lifted her head, Connor had an unreadable expression on his face. "Don't you have to teach him how to be a cyborg?" she asked.

"It is traditionally a communal experience. It will be different doing that, given our current circumstances." Connor sighed. "He'll need somewhere to stay where he can be in close contact with others, should he have questions his programming can't answer. We can get him set up in a house close to mine, once more houses have been constructed."

New Eden expected other people to move to the planet in the coming years, with interest from a species called Dilorans that lived aboard Waystation 8305-C, the nearest commercial hub. The original founders of the settlement had made plans for infrastructure to support hundreds of people, far more than the current population of under fifty. New Eden wanted to be ready to welcome newcomers. "I guess," Pauline said, thinking of her own house, ready to fall down around her ears. She'd been waiting for Aiden to return to her, so they could move into a new one together.

It wasn't going to happen. She knew that now. The man who had walked away from her holding Aiden's clothes, with Aiden's body, wasn't him. She would grieve that realization privately, nurse a whole new kind of pain when she returned home.

"We can be friends, right?" she asked.

Connor blinked. "I thought we were already on friendly terms."

"No, I meant AL17." Success! She hadn't called him Aiden.

"Oh, of course. I'm a medic, not a dictator. I'm not going to interfere with his overtures at friendship. I encourage it."

"I know now he isn't Aiden," she said. "And I know I should have listened to you in the first place. You could be telling me that you told me so, and you haven't."

Connor looked affronted at the suggestion. "My social skills are stunted, but not that badly."

"So are mine," she replied wryly. "The whole planet is full of people with stunted social skills, teamed up with another socially awkward group."

She tried not to remember the first night she and Aiden met. He'd hardly been awkward. On the contrary, he was direct, his flirtations smooth. She'd fallen head over heels for him immediately.

Do not think about that. That part of my life is gone and is never coming back.

"Even so, I like to believe that I possess at least a passable bedside manner when it comes to humans. James would tell me otherwise," Connor said.

"Yeah, he's not the kind of person who keeps his opinions to himself."

Connor grinned, revealing perfect teeth. It was a rare sight and transformed his face. "He is not. He is one of the rare people who can balance truth and sensitivity in his interactions with others. Remarkable for someone who was isolated for so long."

"He had a long time to think things through." Pauline glanced down the corridor. "I don't think AL17 is coming back."

Connor's eyes went blank, the metallic pupils going white, a terrifying sight to anyone who was unfamiliar with how the cyborgs communicated over their shared broadcast link. "He requires my help," he said, his eyes returning to normal.

My help. Not *our* help. Despite her acknowledging that Aiden was truly dead, sadness wound through her. "Go help him. I'm going to head home, get some rest." She had no idea what time it was, only that the suns were out. She hadn't been able to keep track of time for months. With a sigh, she said, "I'll see you later."

CHAPTER SIX

AL17 FOUND suitable undergarments and a pair of boots in the storage lockers belowdecks, near a cargo bay that his sensors told him was half-full of crates. He was dressed when CW44 appeared. *I see you found everything.*

AL17 nodded. It was very well organized. *What is my assigned task for today?*

CW44 blinked. AL17's eyes scanned the other cyborg's expression, interpreting it as confused. *Why would you expect to work today?*

Now it was AL17's turn to be confused. *Why would I not? Is this not my purpose?*

CW44 sighed and closed his eyes for a few seconds. Why, AL17 couldn't tell. *I suppose all of us emerged from our tanks ready to work. It didn't occur to me that we should rewrite that part of the programming.*

How would you remove the impulse to make oneself useful? Isn't that the meaning of our existence?

If you had asked me that six months ago, I would have had a different answer for you. No, being useful is not a purpose in life. There are a great deal of other things to look forward to.

Such as?

Let's go outside and you can meet the others. CW44 turned around and left the storage room, AL17 following closely behind. Aloud, CW44 said, "We prefer to use our physical voices these days. It's considered polite in this society."

Do the humans who live here not want to be cybernetically enhanced?

"Out loud," CW44 reminded him.

An unfamiliar feeling rose in AL17—irritation? He tamped it down. "Do the humans who live here not want to be cybernetically enhanced?"

"Not the way we are, although there is one person who has had some enhancements, due to an illness. This society is rebuilding with our help, in exchange for our living here." CW44 kept speaking as they ascended the stairs. "Your programming will include details about our terraformed habitat on an asteroid in another star system. It's gone now, destroyed in the largest ion storm known in the galaxy."

They walked through a warren of corridors until they reached the exterior airlock. The door was partially open, letting a sliver of sunlight spill across the deck. Intrigued by the sight, AL17 stared at it for a few seconds, eager to see more of this planet.

And Pauline. The thought popped into his head of its own accord. But of course he would want to see her again; she was the first unenhanced human he'd seen. She had stayed at his side while he was generating. He had to be special to her too.

He pulled his gaze away from the sunlight to CW44's face. "I promise to behave as the rest of you do," he said solemnly. "Although I may have questions that my programming cannot answer."

"That won't be an issue. You can ask any one of us for

help." CW44 heaved the door outward. AL17 blinked against the onslaught of sunlight. He'd expected it to be bright, but not like this. "Oh, and you can call me Connor. All of us have taken names outside our designations."

"Where do I get a name?"

CW44—Connor—shrugged. "Some of us have chosen to use the names of our originals, others have picked random names, others were named by their partners or friends."

"What should my name be?" AL17 asked. They stepped into dazzling sunlight. It took a second for his vision to adjust.

"You have plenty of time to decide that, should you take one. Come with me. We can find a house for you."

"Wait. I thought I was supposed to rest in a recharging pod? Does the house not have a pod?" AL17 walked down a ramp, the novelty of being outside pushed aside as he tried to figure out what he was supposed to do next.

"We don't need to recharge in a pod. We can get an equivalent amount of rest sleeping in a bed. It just takes longer."

"But can I return to the ship for rest instead?" His boots landed on overlong grass that was yellowing in spots. "This does not look like a launch site." Looking over his shoulder, he saw the ship rested in what looked like an untended field. His vision registered a comms tower about two hundred meters away, a smaller version of the cyborgs' ship docked at a launch pad in front of it. One hundred meters in front of him, he could see a small settlement. A mix of buildings populated the area, some looking like they were ready to fall over.

"Of course, you can return. You just aren't obligated to. And no, this isn't a launch site. There wasn't one when we arrived."

The settlement's juxtaposition of decay and newness was jarring, even to someone recently activated like him. It would be worth exploring in his spare time, once he found out how he was supposed to be productive. Searching his memory banks, he located a couple of maps of the settlement. The files were made months apart, the first showing decrepit structures sparsely arranged around the settlement; the other was more recent.

He honed in on a small house on the settlement's west side. *Atwater house*, he mentally cataloged. *Pauline lives there.*

Blinking, the map's image evaporated in front of his eyes. How had he known whose house it was? They weren't labeled. Yet in a muddle of peeling white-tiled roofs, he'd noticed that one immediately.

It must be a residual memory from my last iteration. He shrugged it off. The house didn't mean anything to him.

Did it?

———

HE STILL HADN'T BEEN TOLD what he was supposed to do to help this planet rebuild. According to his programming's files, New Eden was a failed isolationist colony, prone to seismic activity. The last major earthquake had been devastating, prompting the planet's *de facto* leader, Hannah Forsyth, to send out an intergalactic SOS that the cyborg contingent intercepted. There had to be an endless amount of work ahead of the settlement, yet no one had said what his role was to be.

I cannot sit idle. Nor did he want to look for a place to live, when he was content to recharge in a pod aboard the starship. Checking the settlement's map again, he noted that the structure closest to him was labeled the agri-center.

He would head there first, see if they required his assistance.

He passed a few unenhanced humans wearing cloth tunics and short pants that were frayed from wear, their faces and limbs tanned by the pair of suns hanging in the sky. Their expressions shifted when they caught sight of him, physically flinching when he nodded his head in their direction.

Had he made a mistake? Wasn't that considered acknowledgement, a polite human custom? He would have to ask someone better versed in unenhanced ways.

The agri-center had a large barn, its doors open, a chicken coop, its boards gray with age, and a modern greenhouse that looked new, surrounded by fields. His nostrils involuntarily constricted when he walked through the barn doors, his sensors alerting him to the presence of cattle. He spied a small cloning unit to his immediate left, its tank empty. Ahead of him was a corridor lined with livestock stalls, a few animal heads peeking out from their tops. To his right was an open space, ramshackle tables arranged haphazardly around the area.

They had packed and processed food here. He had helped. The memory popped into his head unbidden. It must have been from his previous iteration. Shaking his head, as if to dislodge the memory, he took a few more steps across the floor, strewn with pieces of hay and bits of feed. "Hello?"

A door on the far side of the open area opened, something he hadn't noticed immediately. One of the women who was there at his activation stuck her head out. *Hannah Forsyth*, his internal comp reminded him. Eyes widening in surprise, she exclaimed, "Hey! What are you doing up?"

Why was everyone so concerned about his being

awake? "Good day," he replied. "I'm here to perform labor."

She blinked, not replying for a few seconds. "You want to start working right away?"

"You are the leader of this settlement, aren't you? Is it not your responsibility to assign work?"

"I don't exactly consider myself the leader, but if you're looking for something to do?" She looked around the barn. "We're on top of everything food-wise, thank God. Uh—what about the power plant?" Before he could form a reply, she muttered to herself, "No, they have everything under control there." Louder, she said, "The seismology center. It's brand new, and they're looking for someone else to learn how to monitor everything. The seismology center is on the northwest side of the settlement."

"Was that what AL16 was assigned to do before he expired?"

Hannah flinched, paling under her tan. "He was doing a lot of stuff before he…before he passed. Please, do us all a favor and don't use the word 'expired' when referring to Aiden. Especially around Pauline Atwater."

His heartbeat picked up speed at the mention of her name. "The woman who was there when I was activated," AL17 replied. The memory of her sad face came to mind. "She and AL16 were companions, were they not?"

"Something like that. Look, just don't say 'expired' around her, and I'm sure you'll both be fine. Or sort of fine."

AL17 nodded. He was curious about the kind of relationship AL16 and Pauline once had that garnered such reactions from everyone, but he didn't press the issue. If his sensors were correct, Hannah was nervous about passing on those details. "I will refrain from awkward topics of discussion," he promised. "Thank you for the advice about the seismology center. I remember Pauline mentioned they may be looking for extra help. I will go there now."

"Do you know where it is?"

He conjured an image of the settlement's map, zoning in on the northwest corner of the settlement. "I can walk there in fifteen minutes. Three, if I run. Goodbye, Hannah."

Without waiting for another response, he walked out of the barn.

CHAPTER SEVEN

"I thought working here would help." Pauline sighed and leaned back in her seat. The new chair, with its seat that had all of its original padding, was definitely more comfortable than anything she had at home. It was unsettling, in a way. She kept expecting the cushion to split apart or for the chair to groan under her weight from years of overuse.

Lauren Lansing, her fellow volunteer, gave her a sympathetic look from her own seat. "I really want to say it'll get better, but I don't know that for sure."

"I appreciate the empathy, anyway." She stared at the command console in front of her, all of its alerts and buttons glowing a reassuring green. Pauline didn't understand how the machinery worked. Darius had given them an introduction that he made as simple as he could. It could predict an earthquake up to forty-eight hours before it happened, which would give whoever was watching the equipment enough time to send out alerts to the settlement. All Pauline had to do was press a button if anything on the monitors turned red.

Why the hell did I think this job would keep me busy? The new buildings were quake-proof; those that weren't were being rapidly replaced. The disaster three years ago was unlikely to be repeated. All Pauline had to do on a six-hour shift was wait for the console's lights to start flashing red while she was tormented by her memories and thoughts.

"Do you want to talk about it?" Lauren asked.

Pauline shook her head. "No, but thank you for the offer."

"Any time." Lauren shifted in her seat next to Pauline's. "Do these feel weird to you?"

"Yeah. I was just thinking that."

"It's like we expect everything to fall apart as soon as we touch it. Like we don't believe we deserve nice things."

"I was thinking I'd feel more comfortable if I brought one of my old kitchen chairs here. Well, not *comfortable*, exactly…"

"Familiar," Lauren offered.

"Yeah."

A few moments passed in near-silence, punctuated only by the low hum of the machinery before them. A light breeze drifted in from the center's open door, its warmth a relief from the cold temperature of the equipment room. "We should have brought some books," Pauline said.

"What, I'm not fun enough for you?"

Pauline grinned at her, feeling her spirits buoy a little. "Of course you are."

Lauren smiled. "I get it. We'd have more to talk about if we had a book club or something. We should see if Jasmine would loan a couple to us. I bet she would."

Jasmine definitely would. In addition to clothing New Eden, she had been talking about building a library, the first New Eden would have in decades. But thinking about the library reminded Pauline about the discussion regarding the need for a school in a few years and how she was unlikely to have children who would attend it.

She closed her eyes and took a deep breath, pushing away the notion.

"Hey." Lauren touched her arm. "Are you okay? I can keep an eye on all of this if you want to take off for a bit."

Pauline opened her eyes and glanced at the clock installed on the wall opposite them. "We have less than two hours to go. I'm fine, I really am."

"I didn't expect such an essential job to be so boring," Lauren said, echoing Pauline's earlier thought.

"Neither did I. Maybe we should offer to work at the control and comms tower instead."

"I'm sure we have enough cutlery to melt into screws or whatever to fix broken communicators," Lauren said. That was how Hannah had repaired the broadcast equipment in the tower and contacted the cyborg contingent, by melting down a spoon to join a few pieces of it together.

"That's still outside my experience and comfort level. It's probably best if the cyborgs look after that for now."

"Ugh." Lauren leaned back in her seat. "Look at you, being logical. Although I still think bringing some books is a good idea."

"I'll ask Jasmine about it before our next shift." Pauline remembered the last time they'd spoken, and with the memory, a flicker of shame. Jasmine hadn't deserved her ire. It would give her a chance to apologize.

Apologize and then ask her for a favor. The idea made Pauline feel like shit, but she didn't backtrack on her promise.

"She has novels, right? Pick out something interesting for me. All of it—sex, violence, interstellar trav—" Lauren paused, looking at something behind Pauline's shoulder, at the open door.

She didn't have to turn around to recognize the heavy-booted footsteps striding across the floor. Her heart slammed against her ribs, and she took a couple of seconds to collect herself before turning around. "Hi," she said, voice unnaturally high, thanks to nervousness.

AL17 wore an expression that Pauline could only describe as blank curiosity, something most of the others had when they'd first arrived. Most of them had been puzzled about the humans' primitive way of life, how they grieved and fought and celebrated with each other. "Good afternoon," he said, then stood with his arms at his side, the way all the cyborgs had their first night on New Eden, waiting for orders from Rhys.

"Hey," said Lauren. Her gaze flicked between Pauline and AL17. "Um, is there anything we can help you with?"

"I am here to inquire about working."

Oh, no. How the hell was Pauline supposed to heal with the doppelgänger of her dead partner working alongside her? Why had she suggested it in the first place? How the hell could she refuse? She wasn't the president of seismology. "Oh," she said. She caught Lauren's eye, as if the other woman could telepathically tell her how to react to this bit of news. "That's great. It's pretty straightforward. You just look out for lights turning red, and then push one of the blue buttons if it happens. I don't know how the technology works exactly, but, um." She met Lauren's gaze again. Lauren raised a brow, waiting for her to continue. "It's not that hard," she finished.

AL17 nodded, expression shifting to one of concentration. "Has there been any unusual seismic activity recently?"

Pauline couldn't believe she was having this conversation. "There was a minor quake nearly a year ago."

"A couple of months after your group arrived," Lauren

added.

"Yeah. And nothing since. This place was just built. We had to wait until after the rainy season to install everything. Well, not *we*. I have no idea how it works. But your cyborg friends do, and they took care of it."

AL17 opened his mouth, as if to offer a response, thought better of it, and closed it. "Understood."

"But if you want to work here, you're welcome to," Pauline offered.

"Really?" murmured Lauren.

Pauline shot her a look. "We don't have the authority to refuse."

"Who would have that authority?" AL17 asked, appearing unperturbed at the brief exchange between the two women.

"Darius and Tommy are taking care of the seismology stuff, but I doubt they'd ban you from working here," Pauline said.

"It would make sense for me to work here. I do not require the same amount of rest unenhanced humans do, so I can work more hours, and the programs for this equipment have already been uploaded into my internal computer. I believe I am an ideal candidate for this work."

Pauline and Lauren exchanged another glance. "You don't have to convince us that you're qualified," Pauline said. He had come out of his tank, already knowing how the universe worked.

"Excellent." AL17 moved a few steps closer to Pauline, then stood in front of the console, hands clasped behind his back. From her vantage point, she couldn't see his eyes but knew he had to be looking at each light in turn, waiting for something to change color.

"You're starting now?" Lauren asked incredulously.

"Of course. What else would I do?"

"Do you want a chair?" Pauline asked, motioning to stand.

He surprised her when he touched her shoulder, halting her before she could rise to her feet. She felt his touch as acutely as a brand, unexpectedly drawing the breath from her lungs. A bolt of heat shot through her, familiar and unwelcome.

Looking up, she saw his gaze fixed on her, his expression intense. His eyes were blue, the same color as Aiden's. For a few seconds, he reminded her of him so much that she fell back against her seat, legs weak.

"No," he replied, his eyes not leaving her face. "Standing isn't a hardship." Moving his hand, he again clasped them behind his back and resumed staring at the console. "Please don't stop your conversation on my account. I believe I heard you discussing books before I arrived."

"Oh, yeah. I guess we'll get some from Jasmine the next time we're here to help pass the time faster."

"Why are there two of you?" AL17 asked. "This monitoring equipment does not require the presence of two people."

"Of course it does," Lauren said. "If something happens, and there's one person here who tends to freak out and freeze when something starts beeping and flashing red, no one will be notified about an earthquake in time."

"New Eden's buildings have seismic monitors. The inhabitants would be notified," AL17 replied, puzzled.

"There also isn't enough work to go around for everyone right now," Pauline added.

"And this work, in particular, gets lonely," Lauren said.

"Understood." AL17 resumed staring at the green lights.

A moment passed in silence. Pauline and Lauren

glanced at each other. Lauren half shrugged, as if to say she had no idea what to do next. Pauline shared the sentiment.

"Do not stop talking on account of my presence," AL17 reminded them.

They hadn't been talking about him before he arrived, yet Pauline wasn't sure how to bring up a subject as innocuous as novels with him in the room, knowing he would probably be full of questions. Why hadn't he gone back to the starship to recharge in a pod like Connor suggested? Or sought out other cyborgs?

He was looking for you.

No. She tamped down that notion. AL17 didn't know who she was, who she had been to Aiden. He had been cloned into an entirely new person who had to learn how to live on an unfamiliar planet with unfamiliar people. Besides that, she could not let herself think of such possibilities if she wanted to keep her heart from shattering again.

"I'll ask Jasmine for a couple of books," Pauline promised.

————

AL17 WAS FROZEN IN PLACE, unable to bring himself to look at Pauline Atwater for fear of giving away his thoughts. When he'd placed his hand on her shoulder, the memory of her assailed him—next to her, in a bed that wasn't quite big enough for both of them, naked bodies covered by a threadbare sheet. Her head was settled against his shoulder, his arms wrapped around her. It had lasted for all of a second, and he replayed that memory over and over as he stared at the green lights.

Where the hell had that come from?

CHAPTER EIGHT

It was early evening when Pauline found herself in front of the house Jasmine shared with her partners. It was a newly built pre-fab home, built on the site where Jasmine's old house once stood, next door to Hannah and Rhys's house. The small front yard had a few flowering plants, grown from off-world seeds. A blue metal chaise and a pair of lawn chairs with matching seat cushions completed the look. White curtains adorned the front windows, hiding the house's interior from prying eyes.

Pauline took a deep breath and knocked on the door. Jasmine opened it, eyes widening in surprise when she saw who her visitor was. "Hey."

"Hi." Pauline shifted, resisting the urge to look at her feet. "I'm sorry I was rude today. And all the time. I know I've been difficult lately." Maybe she should apologize now and come back another time to ask to borrow a couple of books.

"It's okay."

"No, it isn't. I've been taking out my grief on everyone,

and that isn't fair. It's a small planet. We have to get along."

"Yeah." Jasmine glanced behind her. "Do you want to come in?"

May as well be polite. "Sure." Pauline stepped into the foyer. "This is a nice place." The foyer walls were colored a peach shade, reminding Pauline of what the twin suns looked like when they were setting. A holo of her, Simon, and Darius was displayed in a frame on the wall, along with a few pictures of landscapes drawn in colored pencils, signed with Darius's name.

Their black and white kitten, Jelly, wandered into the foyer, wrapping her tail around Jasmine's bare leg and mewed. "You have another hour before I'm supposed to feed you," Jasmine said to the cat. To Pauline, she asked, "Do you want some water or something?"

"Actually, I came by to ask to borrow something."

"Oh, you're here for books." Jasmine seemed unperturbed by the reason for the visit. "Everyone's coming here for books. Sure, I have a bunch in the living room."

A bunch was an understatement. At least a dozen crates filled the living room, all of them open and full of neatly arranged books. "Where did all these come from?" Pauline asked in wonderment.

"Remember the supply run some of the guys made when the rainy season ended?" Pauline nodded. "They brought these back from Waystation 8305-C. We have a good start on the library's catalog."

"We have plenty for everyone now."

"Yeah, but people will probably be moving to New Eden soon, after more houses are built. We'll need a school too, although I have no idea how we're going to teach kids, but…" Jasmine threw up her hands and smiled. "I won't be teaching. I'm not taking that on."

Pauline forced herself to smile, even though talking about future children was painful. Changing the subject, she said, "Lauren and I are looking for a couple of books to read during our shifts at the seismology center."

"Sure. How's that going, by the way? I haven't been there since the building went up and we moved out of the old Millman place."

"It's boring as shit, but that's probably a good thing."

"Which is why you need something fun to read." Jasmine looked over the sea of cartons. "Do you have a particular theme in mind? I have some old world reprints that are supposed to be classics, although they look pretty dry to me, and I have trouble reading the old spellings." She picked up a hardcover book with disdain. "Ollie likes them."

"Ollie reads for fun?" New Eden's oldest resident had hated everything and everyone until the Si'laar showed up, when he promptly befriended Korjek, their leader. The pair of them enjoyed sitting on Ollie's porch and complaining together.

"Yeah, he likes old pirate books. What are you in the mood for?"

"Something that isn't sad and is written in a version of Standard that we can follow." They had discovered when the cyborgs landed that the entire planet was speaking a language dialect that no longer existed elsewhere in the universe.

"I have something that'll work." Jasmine hopped over a crate and lifted the lid of another. "Tommy was kind enough to have some book files translated into something close enough to our Standard when they were on the waystation. You said you don't want anything sad, but what about scary?"

"How scary?"

Jasmine picked up a paperback book and opened the cover, reading the summary inside. "Ghosts?"

Pauline stiffened. She was working with a kind of ghost at the seismology center, wasn't she? "Not ghosts."

"Uh." Jasmine pawed through the stack of books inside. "Vampires?"

"What's a vampire?"

"An old world legend about monsters who eat human blood, but it looks like a few cultures have stories about them. I have books about a Diloran vampire who lives in trees. They call them 'gatricks.' I'm probably mispronouncing that."

Jelly the kitten jumped on one of the boxes, landed on the books, and promptly jumped out.

"The gatrick books sound good for us."

Jasmine removed a pair of books with red covers and held them out. "There's a whole series about this gatrick who stalks and eats people, but only serial killers. They have this theme about morals and desires, I'm not sure. Darius read them and said they're pretty good." She lifted the lid of another carton, hesitating before speaking again. "Do you want a blank journal?"

"I have some paper at home." She had every love note she and Aiden had exchanged with each other, kept in a small box under her bed.

"That's the homemade stuff that keeps getting re-made over and over." Jasmine removed a slim volume with a gold cover and handed it to Pauline. "Open that."

Tucking the novels under her arm, Pauline did so. The paper inside was blank, perfectly white and smooth. "Wow." She ran her fingers over it. It seemed a shame to write on something so flawless.

"Yeah, it's beautiful, isn't it? You can keep it."

Pauline's breath caught. "Are you sure? This looks valuable."

"You'd be surprised. Hardly anyone outside New Eden seems to use paper or read paper books. I found a place at the waystation that had tons of them, and Tommy said he got these for a steal. They're antique. They've been in storage for forever, and he said the vendor wanted to get rid of them."

Pauline clutched the book to her chest, not knowing how badly she wanted something like this until she had it in her hands. "Thank you."

"Take this too." Jasmine held out a bottle of ink. "Do you still have a refillable pen?"

"Yeah, it's been in the family for years."

"And probably out of ink for almost as long."

Pauline nodded. Her father had once used a mix of animal blood and vegetable juice to create his own ink. *Ugh.* "Thank you."

"The library should be up and running by the time you're finished with the novels, so you can bring them back there," Jasmine said. Looking around the crowded living room, she put her hands on her hips and sighed. "I'll be glad to get these out of here. I keep finding new things to read, and then nothing else gets done."

Pauline smiled. "Thank you again."

"You're welcome. I'm glad people are finding fun things to do. Does that sound weird?"

"Not at all. I'm glad people are letting themselves be happy." To her relief, Pauline's reply didn't come out sounding bitter.

There must have been something in her voice or her expression that gave her away. Jasmine tilted her head, giving her a questioning look. "I'm not going to ask if you're okay, but…"

"AL17 showed up at the seismology center today, looking for work."

Jasmine's mouth dropped open in surprise. "Oh, shit. Why didn't you start with that when you walked in?"

"I didn't want to unload on you. I came here to apologize and ask to borrow books. And I have to get used to seeing him around the settlement. I was polite to him." The memory of his hand on her shoulder, innocent as it was, still made her stomach quiver.

"You could work in the library with me," Jasmine said, but Pauline shook her head.

"I have to learn how to live with him," she replied firmly. "We've been through awful, weird shit before. I can get through this too."

"You don't have to work anywhere you…"

"I know." Pauline hoped her voice brooked no argument. "Look, I want to keep working there. There's enough fail safes built into the equipment that I can't break anything. Lauren's there. It's close enough to my house." *For now*, she mentally added. Sooner rather than later, her house would have to come down and be replaced with something that could withstand an earthquake. Just because it hadn't fallen down during the big one three years ago didn't mean it could survive a repeat event.

"I can ask around about finding something else for him," Jasmine said.

"He said there's nothing else he can do. The agricenter's staffed, the power station is online, so is the comms tower. We're actually pretty efficient." An uncharacteristic wave of pride washed over Pauline when she thought about how New Eden had improved.

"Maybe when we open up to intergalactic trade, he can help with that," Jasmine offered. "Dilorans from the waystation want to move here, remember. There are probably others looking for somewhere quiet and out of the way to raise a family."

Once upon a time, Pauline had looked forward to new arrivals, seeing her community expand. She reminded herself that she should still look forward to that. "That might be a good idea," she agreed, keeping her answer vague.

"If you change your mind about the seismology center…"

"I'll look into working at the library. Thank you for the offer."

Jelly meowed from somewhere in the house. "She's not going to let up until I feed her," Jasmine said with a sigh.

"She's cute enough to make up for the noise."

"She is, and she's totally in love with Simon, even though I picked her out. I mean, I get it, I'm in love with him too. But what a kick in the teeth, right?"

"Yeah," she said, knowing Jasmine was expecting a response. Forcing herself to smile, she said, "Thank you again for everything."

———

BACK AT HER HOUSE, Pauline pulled the small wooden box from underneath her bed. It had been in her family for generations, brought to New Eden from the old world. Gingerly opening the lid, she lifted out a few rough scraps of homemade paper, gray and mottled yellow in places. She knew the words of all the notes by heart, but she re-read them, anyway.

You are brighter than any star in the universe. Is that corny? I bet you'll tell me after you read this.

Last night was the best ever. I bet tonight will top that.

Turns out that love at first sight isn't a stupid fairy tale. I love you, Pauline Alice Atwater.

Pauline tucked a few of the notes in the back pages of the journal. Turning to the first page, she marveled over the paper's smoothness for a moment, in awe that something so perfect and precious was unwanted by the rest of the universe. She dug around her bedside table for her pen and refilled it with the ink Jasmine had given her, taking care not to spill it on the unmade sheets. Nib hovering over the paper for a moment, she began to write.

One year ago, New Eden was on the brink of death. Rescue arrived in the form of cyborgs. One of them was the love of my life, and now that he has died, I have to look at him every day.

CHAPTER NINE

New Eden's twin suns had long dipped below the horizon by the time AL17 was relieved of his duties at the seismology center. He'd been all but chased away by Tommy and a member of a four-armed species who introduced themself as Tibbot. Held in Tibbot's lower arms was a small bundle wrapped in a silvery heatsaver. A pair of tiny, green-scaled arms poked out, clinging to Tibbot's shipsuit. AL17's sensors quickly analyzed the pair, reporting back that they were a member of the Si'laar, a species that was nearly extinct and reproduced asexually by cloning in a way that was very similar to AL17's reproduction. "You are Si'laar," AL17 announced.

"I see Connor's tweaks to your programming were effective," Tommy remarked. He slid into the same seat Pauline had occupied earlier in the day.

The memory of her made his heart skip a beat for the second time since his activation. Making a note to himself to run a cardiac diagnostic when he returned to the starship for recharging, he replied, "I have dossiers on all the species who live on New Eden."

Tibbot sat next to Connor. The bundle strapped to their chest shifted, a bird-like squawk escaping from it. "They will settle down soon," Tibbot said.

Curiosity had AL17 looking at them more closely. "A baby?"

"Yes. Mine," Tibbot said proudly. Their golden-scaled face beamed with pride, a single white eyebrow lifting. "They were born two weeks ago. The first to my unit since my own birth."

He was supposed to congratulate someone when they had a new offspring. A half-buried point of etiquette surfaced in AL17's mind. "Congratulations," he said. He hoped he wouldn't be expected to hold the baby. That was common in humanoid cultures, wasn't it? Did the Si'laar expect it, too?

Tibbot beamed. "Thank you." They looked down fondly at the baby.

"What is their name?" AL17 asked.

"Their name will not be decided until we hold a naming ritual and the name is revealed to the unit," Tibbot said.

"There's been some friction with the way Tibbot wants to raise their baby and the rest of the clan," Tommy explained. "I've heard all about it in our poker game."

Tibbot adjusted the baby against their chest. "Korjek has strong opinions."

"Yeah, it's why they get along so well with Ollie." Tommy surveyed the room, to the solid green lights on all the equipment. To AL17, he said, "You can head home. We'll be fine the rest of the night."

"Monitoring for seismology changes will not interfere with Tibbot's child rearing?"

"No," Tibbot replied. "I look forward to interactions with my friends in the evenings."

"Right back at you," Tommy said fondly.

Watching their exchange made AL17 feel awkward, an interloper in their friendship. In the background of his mind, his processor provided details on Si'laar infancy and the naming ritual, which would occur when the baby was the equivalent of six weeks old, and then defined poker as a card game originating on the planet Earth. In the forefront, he didn't know how to extricate himself from this situation without making it more awkward. "When am I expected to return here?" he asked.

Tommy shrugged. "Tomorrow afternoon?"

The answer came out as a question, like Tommy had no idea how such an important facility should be staffed. But it was likely the only one AL17 would get. "I will return tomorrow afternoon. Will Pauline be here too?"

Tommy and Tibbot stilled. Had AL17 made a misstep? He was looking forward to seeing her again, sad as she was. "Pauline isn't scheduled for another shift for a couple of days," Tommy finally replied.

"And you will be here in the morning?"

"No, I'll be doing a few hours' worth of work in the hospital while Connor gets some rest," Tommy explained.

An image of the two cyborgs flashed in AL17's mind, but it wasn't taking place on New Eden. They were on a desert planet, the sky blazing orange under the heat of a vicious sun, surrounded by sandy hills. AL17 lay on his back in excruciating pain while the two of them checked his vitals. All three of them wore identical black flight suits and helmets. He shook his head, dislodging it. It must be from one of his previous iterations.

"Are you okay?" The look on Tommy's face was one of concern.

"I'm fine. Why do you ask?" Despite the affirmation,

something still unsettled AL17 about what he had just experienced.

"You kind of blanked out there for a couple of seconds."

The vision had lasted four point three seconds, but AL17 didn't point that out. "It isn't anything to be concerned about. My cybernetics are functioning as they should."

"Was it a flashback from a previous iteration? Rhys calls them 'memory shards,' but they're the same thing." Tommy's expression turned serious. "You can talk about them, you know. We all have them from time to time."

"I was lying prone in the sand in a desert in searing heat." The words left AL17 before he could reconsider them, coming out in a rush. *Why had I done that?* "I was in severe pain. You and Connor were there in previous iterations."

Tommy's brows lifted a little, an expression AL17 analyzed as surprised. "That sounds horrible. I'm sorry you had to see that."

"Is that scenario unfamiliar to you?"

Tommy nodded. "I don't recall any time spent in a desert environment, and I'm not sure I care to. New Eden is hot enough for me."

AL17 had the notion that Tommy was trying to make a joke, although it didn't seem to have a punchline. Perhaps he was attempting to lighten the mood by reminding everyone of their shared circumstances? AL17 didn't have any other climates to compare New Eden's to.

Was Tommy waiting for a reply? "Mm," said AL17 noncommittally. He hoped that would suffice.

"I think all of us have those memories surface from time to time," Tommy explained. "If it happens frequently or the visions last more than a few seconds, tell me or

Connor. Probably Connor first, since he's the most knowledgeable medic we have right now. We don't want another situation like Rhys's."

The mention of the cyborg leader piqued AL17's interest. "What type of situation?"

"Rhys had some faulty hardware in his head that caused repeated memory shards to resurface for extended periods. We had to essentially revive him, and the surgery was rather gruesome." Tommy's lips thinned. "You were cloned without any of the components Rhys had. I don't expect that to happen again, but you should be aware of the symptoms."

Tibbot's baby stirred. "Do you want a break?" Tommy asked. "I can take them off your hands for a bit."

The Si'laar's lower arms wrapped around the baby in a protective gesture. "Both of us are comfortable for now."

"Offer's open if you need it."

Tibbot beamed. "Thank you."

Something pulled at AL17, an internal reminder that it was time for him to leave. "Have a pleasant evening," he said, hoping that was polite. He tried to smile and nodded his head before turning around and leaving the building.

Walking into the cool night air was oddly refreshing. He waited until he was far enough away from the seismology center, so there was no chance of Tommy and Tibbot seeing him, before he stopped on the path, taking in his surroundings. He could hear the gentle waves of the sea on the west side of the settlement, where the Si'laar slept away the days. The fragrances of grass, trees, and new buildings mingled with each other. He spotted a cluster of older homes in the distance close to the seashore, lights burning in the windows that were still intact. He wondered why the houses were still standing when new ones were available.

Without any place to go, other than the starship, he began walking again, his pace slower. Without the daytime bustle, he was free to look around the settlement without being gawked at as a man returned from the dead, a poor facsimile of whoever AL16 had been.

He'd been liked, AL17 realized with a start. He'd had friends among the cyborgs and New Edeners, possibly the Si'laar, depending on how long they had been here since his previous iteration's death. And he had found love with Pauline Atwater, the same woman who had been on AL17's mind since she left the seismology center after her shift.

He kept walking and, to his surprise, found himself in front of a ramshackle house in a section of the settlement that hadn't been redeveloped yet. It was two stories, leaning slightly to the left. Hardly a safe place to live long term, he reasoned. And yet the sight of it was oddly comforting. Like he had been there before.

He remained rooted to the spot, palms sweating and heartbeat picking up. He had a pretty good idea whose house this was, why he had been drawn here. But he couldn't bring himself to move up the house's overgrown path and knock at its splintered wooden door.

To his surprise, the door opened and a figure stepped out, holding a flashlight. Its beam shone directly into AL17's face. His ocular enhancements immediately responded, shifting so he could clearly see Pauline's face. The light shook, then went dark as it crashed to the porch.

"What are you doing here?" she asked, her voice edged with panic. She bent down and retrieved the flashlight but didn't move from the porch.

"I finished my shift at the seismology center and was returning to the starship," he replied.

"The ship's that way." Pauline aimed the flashlight

behind her, in the general northeast direction. "Are you lost?"

"I can't get lost. Topographical and geographic maps have been programmed into me, and I—"

"Of course they have been," muttered Pauline.

"I did not mean to frighten you," AL17 replied.

She didn't respond immediately. He couldn't read her expression—not for lack of light, but lack of experience. After a moment, she finally said, "I know."

"But I did."

"In a few ways."

Alarm flared through him. "Truly?"

"Forget I said that. It's complicated."

He pretended to do so, even though this conversation would be forever imprinted in his memory. "Are you returning to the seismology center? Tommy and Tibbot said you weren't expected to come back for another couple of days, although they weren't specific about what they consider to be 'a couple.' I know the definition can vary, depending on dialect or culture."

"Two days," she said. "I'm supposed to go back in two days. 'A couple' means the same thing here as I'm sure it does aboard your ship. And I'm not going back right now. I can't sleep, and I was going to take a walk to clear my head."

"Would you like an escort?" he asked impulsively.

The flashlight quivered in her hand again, but she didn't drop it. "What?"

"An escort," he repeated. "Perhaps for safety?" Even as he said the words, he knew how foolish they were. New Eden didn't have any predators, fauna or otherwise.

"Are you serious?" she asked.

He nodded.

"Would you be offended if I said no?"

"No." Hurt, maybe. But he wouldn't tell her that.

Another moment stretched out between them while he waited for her answer. Was her question his cue to leave her alone? Should he bid her good night and return to the recharging pod aboard the ship? Suddenly, the idea felt very lonely.

"Okay," she said. She stepped off the porch, down the stoop's two stairs, their creaks ominous to AL17's enhanced ears. The whole house needed to be torn down and rebuilt. Surely, it wasn't safe to live in.

She stood in front of him, the flashlight lowered. He remembered that his eyes were on night vision mode, making them glow, another reminder to her of what he was. He blinked away their light so they would appear normal to her.

"Why did you do that?" she asked, echoing his thoughts.

"I thought it would be less unsettling."

"It isn't your eyes that's unsettling to me," she said.

His answer was flat. "It's my resemblance to AL16."

"Yes."

"I feel like I should apologize."

She shook her head. "Don't. It's a fucked-up situation all around. I don't want you to feel bad for existing." She pointed at the main path that meandered through the settlement. "Let's walk."

CHAPTER TEN

Pauline's heart thundered against her ribs, so hard she was sure AL17 could hear it. *Let's walk.* She couldn't believe she had said that. A curious mix of anxiety, grief, and curiosity flowed through her, strong enough that she didn't want to ignore it. AL17 may have rejected her, may not have known who she had been to his previous clone, but they still shared a community. They had to get along with each other.

None of this is his fault. He's trying to be friendly.

"Where do you want to go?" she asked.

He gave a very Aiden-like shrug before replying. "I did not have a destination in mind, other than the starship. Where were you planning to walk to?"

Usually, Pauline wandered along the edges of the settlement—the waterfalls around the power station, the comms tower and newly built launch pad, the field where the cyborgs' ship was docked, sometimes along the beach on its western edge. Places that were usually abandoned in the middle of the night, while the rest of the settlement slept. Or stayed up late complaining about everyone younger than them and playing cards, as Ollie and Korjek were wont to do on Ollie's porch, but they always left Pauline alone when they saw her wandering, save for polite waves in greeting.

She pointed in the direction of the beach. "That way."

He nodded and stayed at her side, his long stride matching her shorter one. Neither of them spoke for a few minutes, and she found she was dying to know what he was thinking. To her surprise, he spoke first. "Do you frequently experience insomnia?"

"Yes." There was no point in lying about it.

"Why don't you speak to Connor? He may be able to help."

She shook her head. "I doubt it. It isn't because of anything physical." Unless one counted a broken heart as physical, but he probably didn't. Besides that, she didn't want to keep on bothering Connor over her troubles.

"Do you want to talk about it?" he asked, surprising her further.

Her breath caught for a couple of seconds, and it took longer than that to form an answer. "Yes. No. I'm grieving," she finally said.

"For AL16?"

"Yes."

He hesitated before speaking again. "I've been informed that you two were companions."

"More than that."

AL17 didn't reply right away. They walked along the path that would take them past the cemetery. How had they managed to make that turn without Pauline noticing? That was the long way to the seaside. Aiden was buried in that cemetery.

"Was he your lover?" he asked curiously.

There was no point in denying it, yet it took Pauline a couple of seconds to reply. "Yeah."

"Did you expect me to be him?"

She didn't know whether she wanted to have this conversation, but she suspected she needed to. *If nothing else, maybe I'll finally get some fucking sleep after I do.* "I did, even though I shouldn't have."

AL17 didn't speak for a few minutes. The only sound was their feet on the ground, hers in her old, flimsy sandals slapping against her heels and his muffled by his black boots. Aiden had taken to dressing like a local in the weeks before he died, she remembered.

"I knew better, but I didn't believe it," she continued, surprising herself. "I just thought—well, Connor and everyone said they made improvements to cloning techniques, and they started cloning Aiden so quickly after he died that I thought you—that he might remember me."

They were approaching the cemetery. To her eternal gratitude, AL17 didn't say anything about it, just followed her lead and continued walking along the path's fork that led to the beach. "You were outside the tank while I was generating." His words were a statement, an affirmation of something he already knew.

Pauline's stomach turned over. "You remember that?"

"I do."

The fleeting thought that he might remember their time together raced through her mind, but she didn't dare voice it. "I hope I made it a little less lonely for you." Had he noticed the way her voice cracked at the end?

"Growth is a solitary process." He sounded puzzled.

"I mean, the rest of you grew and hatched together. I know 'hatched' isn't the right term," she hastily added before he could correct her. "The other cyborgs knew each other right away and could get used to being alive together. You didn't."

"I've received guidance from the others."

"Is it the same thing, though?" She'd never asked him a personal question before. She hoped it wasn't overstepping.

He was quiet again, mulling over an answer. "I supposed that's why I feel like I don't quite fit with the others."

They continued walking, the gentle sound of the sea's waves growing louder as they did so. Pauline wasn't sure how to continue the conversation, how much more either of them could open up to each other. So, she waited for him to elaborate, occasionally kicking a stone out of the way as they meandered along, her flashlight bobbing along the path.

"That makes a lot of sense," AL17 said.

"What does?" Had he been thinking about his reply in his head and forgotten that he hadn't voiced it? Was something in his brain's computer failing? "Are you all right?"

"I'm as all right as I can be. It wasn't until we started talking that I realized the reason I feel so off-kilter isn't because I'm a brand-new iteration. It's because I'm a single iteration with a group of cyborgs who already know each other. I suppose I should be grateful to you for that breakthrough." He inclined his head at her, the metallic bits in his eyes sparkling in the darkness. "Thank you, Pauline."

"You don't have to thank me."

"I do. This is one of the only conversations I've had with someone that isn't superficial, inane chatter about where I should work and how I feel. When I was activated, I identified other cyborgs and assumed we would work in sync because that's what my instincts said should happen. I was ready to be a fighter pilot again and assumed everyone else would be prepared for their programmed roles too. I was surprised when it didn't feel as I expected. And now I know why." He spoke the words matter-of-factly, without a trace of hurt or sadness. "Yet I remember you speaking to me outside the tank after my organs and nerves could process auditory sensations. I was curious."

She'd been so preoccupied with his realizations about himself that she'd nearly forgotten that he remembered her. Not only that, but he'd been curious. "Did you think I was a cyborg?"

"No. I didn't know who you were, only that you were present and appeared to care for me, based on your words. I didn't understand why."

Pauline didn't realize she had been hopeful about his memories of her until they were dashed by his reply. "Oh."

He blithely continued. "If I upset you after I was activated, I apologize. While it wasn't my intention, I understand that the outcome doesn't change how you may have felt. AL16 was very important to you."

"Aiden," she murmured. Part of her was processing his acknowledgement that intentions didn't always affect outcomes. It was sort of refreshing to hear that level of emotional maturity from someone who was effectively a few days old.

"Yes. AL16's chosen name and the one you referred to me by when you were waiting outside the tank."

A lump filled her throat. It took a couple of seconds for her to speak around it. "Yeah. We picked it together. His original's name was Adrian, and he didn't want to use it."

"Some of the other cyborgs have used their originals' names."

"Some do, some don't. It comes down to preference. I don't think there's a right or wrong way to decide."

They were nearly at the beach, the smell of water in the air. The grass was giving way to the tiny pebbles that covered the shore. On especially warm nights, Pauline would shuck her sandals and walk in the water, waves lapping at her ankles, but she kept them on tonight. AL17 seemed the sort to lecture her about the dangers of swimming in the dark if she got closer to the water. Not that she had ever swum at night, having those dangers drilled into her head as soon as she could walk, but he didn't know that.

"Do you think my place is here?" AL17 asked as they approached the beach.

She hadn't been expecting that question. "What do you mean?"

"Would it be more appropriate for me to leave New Eden and look for a life elsewhere?"

For some odd reason, the thought of him leaving pulled at her long-bruised heartstrings. "No!" Her reply came out harsher than she intended. Softening her tone, she asked, "Where would you go, anyway? What do you know about the universe outside New Eden?"

"I've been programmed with the collective knowledge of my cyborg brethren. I'm capable of flying many kinds of ships and shuttles, working on infrastructure projects, or joining a military force, among other abilities."

The notion was absurd. "No, you can't leave." Before he could argue, she amended her point. "You *shouldn't* leave. You guys might still have people pissed off at your originals or another previous generation, and they could be on the lookout for you. It isn't safe."

But even as she said the words, she knew they rang false. While they had kept to themselves prior to emigrating to New Eden, the cyborgs were certain no one was out to settle a centuries-old grudge between them and anyone they'd wronged in the past. *Fairly* certain, she amended. The universe was a huge place.

And AL17 could get lost or hurt in it, his programming be damned.

His response was flat. "You don't want me to leave."

"No."

"But my appearance and mannerisms have upset you. You have no reason to want me to stay here when I'm not your dead lover, and yet my very existence reminds you of him."

She cringed inwardly at the bluntness of his words and hoped her reaction didn't show on her face. "I care about other people. I wouldn't want you to run off half-cocked like that. I'm grieving, is all. I've grieved other people and survived, and I'll get through this too." Regardless of his presence, she needed to feel some cold water right now, to take the edge off what she was feeling. She kicked off her sandals and left them on the pebbles, then waded into the water, sighing in relief as it covered her feet.

"It isn't safe to swim," AL17 said, but he made no move toward the water.

Despite the gravity of the situation and her feelings, she grinned. "I'm not." She walked a few strides; he took a few cautious steps closer to her without getting into the water himself. "It's a nice way to cool down. Not all of us are equipped with internal temperature adjusters."

"My cybernetics are not called…"

"Yeah, I know. I'm lumping them all together in the same category. My point is, I get overheated easily, which sucks when you live on a planet that's hot and humid for most of the year." Unlike other New Edeners, Pauline didn't mind New Eden's too-brief rainy season. It was a nice change of pace from the relentless sunshine.

"Is your house not equipped with cooling ability?"

"No. I'm going to be moving house soon, anyway, so the point is moot. The new houses use a system with recycled water for cooling." Catching his quizzical expression in the light of the twin moons overheads, she quickly added, "I have no idea how the system works, so don't ask."

"Why have you stayed in your house if it's so inefficient?"

"It's my home. I've lived there my entire life. My parents lived there, my grandparents, and so on." She and Aiden had also wanted to design their dream home together, or at least design it as much as they could with a pre-fab unit. "A few other people have been dragging their heels on moving too."

"You're very sentimental," AL17 said.

She wasn't sure how to respond to that. "Yeah?" She kept walking, the feel of shifting pebbles under her feet oddly relaxing. AL17 ambled along at her pace, her sandals in his hands, held by the straps.

"It isn't a criticism. I see the appeal of wanting to keep older objects in your possession, particularly in the face of extreme loss."

Pauline's breath stilled for a second. She wondered if he noticed. That was a surprisingly un-cyborg thing to say, along the lines of the way Aiden spoke. He hadn't seen a backwards people when he came to New Eden; he'd seen people who needed some help and understood why some traditions were worth keeping. He'd been human first, enhanced human second. Before she could stop herself, she said, "Thank you for understanding that." Her voice was soft enough that it might be swallowed by the sound of water, audible only to someone with enhanced hearing.

She stepped out of the water and held out her hands for her sandals. Wordlessly, he gave them to her. She looped the straps over her wrists, ready to walk home barefoot to keep the shoes from getting wet. Catching another questioning look from him, she said, "I don't want to wreck the leather more than I already have."

"I can create shoes for you in the ship's hard goods replicator."

Why did the suggestion make her heart skip a beat? She hated having to reject a present, but she knew the ship's limitations on New Eden. "Don't waste fuel for that. I'm fine walking barefoot for a little while."

"Do you think you will be able to sleep now?"

She shrugged. "Maybe. I'm glad we had this talk."

"You won't be afraid of me anymore?"

"I wasn't afraid of you in the first place. Just shocked. And grieving. I'm sorry you feel so out of place with your people. Our people," she corrected herself. She fished her flashlight from her shorts pocket and switched it on, the beam lighting the way for them.

"I hope we can be friends," AL17 said.

Her stomach turned over at the statement. A feeling she couldn't identify swept over her, an odd combination of trepidation and anticipation. How was she supposed to respond to that?

Her voice came out in a croak. "I hope so too."

CHAPTER ELEVEN

AL17'S EYES FLUTTERED OPEN. It took a couple of seconds for him to orient himself and recognize that he was standing inside a recharging pod. The lights around his head slowly cycled on as he regained consciousness, automatically adjusting as his vision functions came online. *Why am I surprised to find myself in a pod? Where else would I be when I need downtime?*

The answer was immediate and unbidden—a bed. Sleeping like an unenhanced human, lying in a bed, limbs tangled in thin, threadbare sheets. Not just his limbs, either. Blinking, he tried to clear the image from his mind. He must have dreamed it during his rest period's REM cycle.

He stepped outside the pod to the metal deck, the sound of his booted feet dully echoing off the walls. It served as a reminder that he was alone. His sensors reached into the ship's comps, looking for signs of life other than his own, and came up empty.

I'm alone here.

Closing his eyes, he tried to conjure the face of the person he'd been in bed with in his dream, coming up blank. All he could recall was a pair of long, slim legs, browned from the sun, draped over his own, which were taking on a tan too. AL17 looked down at his legs, covered in a black shipsuit, never exposed to sunlight. He'd had a flashback while dreaming. *Memory shards*, Rhys called them.

In that moment, he desperately wished there were other cyborgs around to remind him that what he was experiencing was normal. Loneliness pulled at him, a near physical pain. He remembered his last conversation with Pauline in the middle of the night, two days ago now. Remembered his revelation that he didn't fit in with the rest of his enhanced brethren as a newly cloned cyborg. He had no one to stumble around with, no one to bond with as they learned how to be alive.

He'd been in bed with Pauline in his dream. A shudder of pleasure coursed down his spine at the memory of it, making him wish he'd dreamed more about her. What she looked like in the early dawn light, waking from sleep. Happy to see him.

Would she be awake now? He started walking in the direction of the airlock, determined to pay her a visit, then halted when his internal chronometer reminded him that it was 0300 hours. Far too early for an unenhanced human who stuck to normal waking hours. Frustration roiled in him. Why was he awake so early? He'd stepped into the pod all of five hours ago.

He already knew the answer, as he had with knowing what he had dreamed of. He didn't need the rest when he was plugged into the starship like a kitchen appliance. If he slept in a bed like everyone else who had decided to live like a regular human, he would still be resting. It was yet another reminder of how different he was.

I should move into a house. The most recent off-world supply run had brought back enough pre-fab houses to replace everything rundown, with the last of the original houses scheduled to be torn down and replaced over the coming days. Including Pauline's, he recalled. She'd seemed sad over the inevitable replacement, despite the house being unsound. Connor had also pointed one out to him that would be perfect for a single person to live in.

He started walking toward the airlock again, pausing only when he put his hand against the door. It was still the middle of the night; the only people awake would be the Si'laar and whoever was watching the seismology center—Tommy and Tibbot, if AL17 was correctly remembering the schedule.

Pauline had a shift at the center later in the morning. Perhaps AL17 could join her, see if they could open up to each other, like they had the other night. Excitement thrummed through him at the possibility, something that took him a few seconds to identify. There was something about Pauline that drew him to her like... His internal comps tried to come up with a suitable analogy and failed. Perhaps that part of his programming had been missed while he was in the tank.

With a sigh, he opened the airlock door and stepped onto the exterior ramp, taking a few seconds to breathe in the night air. The temperature had dropped overnight, the humidity receding in a temporary reprieve. It was utterly silent in the field where the starship rested, although AL17 suspected that, if he walked by the agri-center, he might hear the sounds of livestock. Striding down the ramp, a burst of energy filled him, a need to move.

AL17 started to run. First through the field to the main path that wound around the settlement in various states of disrepair, nimbly jumping over cracks and broken pieces of pavement. He picked up speed as he raced past the seis-mology center, the door open and spilling light into the darkness. His sensors registered the presence of TM34—Tommy—and Lauren Lansing, Pauline's friend. Odd that she would be awake at this hour. He ran past the western sea and a couple of Si'laar, who waved all four arms at him. AL17 responded in kind, wondering if the gesture was even noticeable at his speed.

He had completed two full laps around the settlement before he found himself in front of Pauline's house again. The windows were dark, the house silent. AL17 stood before it, his sensors grasping for signs of life inside. He moved a few meters closer until he could touch the house's dilapidated siding and concentrated until he registered the presence of a sleeping humanoid female. This close, he could almost hear her breaths, deep and even.

I should resume my run. Perhaps jump into the sea for a swim. Yet he remained rooted to his spot in front of the house.

An image of its interior popped into his mind. He could see the shabby foyer, an old rag rug, its colors faded decades ago, spread out on the floorboards. To the left of the foyer was a kitchen, dominated by a large dented metal sink and water pump. To the right was a sitting room and a flight of stairs that led to the upper level, where the bedrooms and bathroom were located. The largest bedroom was occupied by Pauline. A wooden bed frame sat in the middle of the room, beneath a small window with cracked glass panes, covered by a thin piece of cloth. The bedding was faded and mismatched, and Pauline lay under the sheets, probably naked.

His breathing and heart rate picked up speed as he envisioned her and the house he had never been in, yet knew like the back of his hand. Aiden had slept in that bed with her, had been glad to since the first moment he'd laid eyes on her. Heat and desire coursed through him as the memory shards from a dead man filled his mind.

Heat, desire, and, curiously, shame. *Have I stolen his memories?* Did AL17 even have the right to want her as badly as he did right now? And where did that impulse come from? He hardly knew her.

The door lock is broken. Broken, and she had never bothered to repair it, because who would break into her house, anyway? He could let himself in, perhaps prepare breakfast in her kitchen as a surprise. He had placed one foot on the stoop when he realized that was a ridiculous idea. His programming was supposed to keep him from doing stupid and thoughtless things, and letting himself into the home of a woman whose dead lover provided AL17's DNA qualified as something immensely stupid and thoughtless.

My programming might be faulty. AL17 remembered the terrifying story about Rhys's brain programming failing and the emergency surgery he had undergone. If he was experiencing something similar, he should speak to a medic. He reluctantly forced himself away from the house, then dashed to the hospital.

To his chagrin, it was empty. With a sigh, he walked the short distance to the small white house that Connor currently occupied. Light peeked through the curtains shading a front window, a hopeful sign that AL17 wasn't about to awaken anyone. He concentrated, connecting himself to the link shared by all the cyborgs. Or had been shared at one time; he was the only person connected to it. *Hello?*

Connor replied a few seconds later. *Is everything all right?*

No. I have reason to believe my programming is failing.

There was a pause before Connor replied. *How so?*

Indignation rose in AL17 at the lack of urgency in Connor's response. *I am not thinking rationally.*

Well, you're here asking for help, which is a rational thing to do when one is in medical distress. Are you experiencing any physical symptoms?

His indignation gave way to frustration. *Could you please confirm if I'm all right?*

Connor audibly sighed over the link. *Yes. I'll meet you at the hospital. Give me a few minutes.*

Relief trickled through AL17. Obediently, he walked to the hospital and opened its front door, the lights automatically cycling on. He'd never been in here, having always been treated in the ship's sickbay. He hoped Connor had the appropriate equipment to handle his concerns. He turned into the first patient room he saw and sat on the bed, hands clasped in front of him.

Connor appeared a few moments later. His hair was too short to be mussed from sleep, but his clothes were wrinkled and had clearly been the first things he had thrown on. "I thought you were awake," AL17 said. "My apologies if I woke you."

"It's fine. It's part of the job when one is a medic. Tell me why you're here at this ungodly hour."

AL17 sidestepped the remark about it being an ungodly hour and how, if Connor still used the recharging pods to rest, he would be wide awake now. "I nearly walked into Pauline's house." He felt foolish as he said the words.

One of Connor's eyebrows lifted. "And? Did you go in?"

"No, but I wanted to. I—I knew the entire house when I thought about it. I've never been inside it. I knew she was sleeping and where, and…" He hesitated, stumbling over his next words, what he was about to admit. "I remember that she was very important to Aiden. I think I remember how he felt about her."

Connor didn't reply immediately, only looked away for

a moment in contemplation. Finally, he said, "And you believe your programming is malfunctioning?"

"I shouldn't have impulses to break into someone else's house, let alone the home of a woman who was in an intimate relationship with the dead man whose DNA I was cloned from."

AL17's answer was met with another long silence from Connor. "I don't believe your programming is faulty," he said.

Hope surged in AL17.

"Unfortunately, I do not know any scientific or medical reason as to why you're experiencing such vivid impulses and memories. This is beyond the scope of my experience."

AL17's optimism flagged. His shoulders slumped in defeat.

"All I can say is that memory shards are common to all of us," Connor added.

"What about Rhys? Didn't he experience this too?"

"That was different. His body was shutting down during extended flashback episodes. You're still physically functioning as you should, and you were not generated with the same components as Rhys. They're much improved. Korjek and I tweaked them together."

"But I'm the first person to be cloned with the newer tech. Maybe there was an error in the code or DNA."

Connor's reply was frosty. "There are no errors."

"Then why are the memory shards so intense?"

Connor blanched, an unexpected reaction for someone who was usually so self-assured. "It could be because your cloning occurred so quickly after your previous iteration's death. The Si'laar has also greatly improved on their cloning techniques since our previous iterations stole their original tech. Perhaps it's due to the improvements I made to the genetic sequencing procedure. You're the first of us to have been cloned in this way."

An insane notion grasped AL17, too intense to ignore. "Is it possible I'm Aiden reincarnated?"

Connor blinked in surprise. "Well, we're all reincarnated from our previous iterations, if you want to think about it in a more abstract, spiritual way."

"What if your new cloning technique made a copy of Aiden instead of an entirely new clone? I remember too much of his life in detail too great to dismiss."

Connor waited again before replying, weighing his response. "I don't know."

"You redesigned the program!"

"I improved an existing, successful program," Connor corrected him. "I did not redesign it. I think it's possible that these improvements could have resulted in a greater resemblance to a previous clone's personality and traits. We will have to wait and see if this is what has happened to you."

And attractions, AL17 thought, careful not to voice it either physically or via their shared link. He'd honed in on Pauline remarkably quickly after recovering from generation and activation. But he didn't share all of Aiden's memories of her, something that frustrated him now.

That is incredibly fucked up. Aiden is dead, and you're lusting after his grieving lover. The epithet popped into his head for the first time since he was activated. He should be surprised, yet he wasn't. Swearing was probably something Aiden did. The rest of the cyborgs certainly weren't shy about it.

AL17 could tell that arguing with Connor about the cloning techniques would be unsuccessful. The dark half moons under the other cyborg's eyes also told him that Connor probably wanted to go back to sleep. "That's likely what happened," AL17 agreed. "It's good to know I'm not dying or malfunctioning."

Connor shook his head. "You're not."

"Thank you for checking. And I apologize for hauling you out of bed."

"You're welcome, although the apology is unnecessary."

He took a few steps back. "Thank you again for confirming that there's nothing wrong with my programming. I'll return to the ship."

"Have you reconsidered moving off it?"

"Yes, but I suppose that now is not the time to explore that."

Connor gave him a wry smile. "No, it isn't."

"I hope you get some more sleep."

"I will. Go recharge. You need it."

CHAPTER TWELVE

THE SEISMOLOGY CENTER WAS EMPTY, save for Pauline and her thoughts. Her freshly refilled pen was clutched in her hand, hovering over a blank page in the notebook Jasmine had given her, open on the console before her.

She had spent a couple of hours the night before writing about her grief, her complicated feelings about AL17, their walk together four nights before, the impending demolition and replacement of her house. Journaling had been something she'd enjoyed when she had access to paper before the earthquake, which had been in decreasing supply prior to the cyborgs' arrival. Part of the reason she'd been so engrossed in her journal was the novelty of using something so new and smooth, the feel of her pen's nib flowing over the paper without catching on minute bumps common to sheets of foolscap that had been repeatedly pulped.

The door sliding open had her sitting up straight, slamming the notebook closed. Her breath caught, heart skipping a beat as familiar footsteps sounded behind her. Without turning her head, she said, "Hi, AL17."

He sat in the empty chair next to her. "You're alone."

She set her notebook and pen on the nearest console, making sure to leave the status lights visible. It was probably unnecessary, since if an earthquake was imminent, the place would be screaming with alarms. As it was, the husky note in his voice set off one of her internal alarms, sending an unexpected frisson of heat bolting through her. "Yeah, Lauren said she'd be by later." She was probably with Tommy, but she didn't bother to mention that.

"What's that?" He pointed to the notebook.

"Just a journal. Present from Jasmine." Remembering that he probably didn't know her, she added, "She was there when you were activated. Tan, light blonde hair, slim?"

He nodded, a faraway look in his eyes. They hadn't turned silver, the sign that he was communicating with other cyborgs telepathically, but it was an odd sight all the same. It reminded her of Aiden. Of course it would; he's his clone. "Notes," he murmured.

She stilled. "I'm sorry?"

"We wrote notes." Her stomach turned over at the reply. Before she could ask him what he meant, he quickly added, "You and Aiden wrote notes to each other."

She glanced away, unable to bring herself to look in his eyes. "Yes. How—how did you know that?"

"I just do."

Memory shards, of course. Just a very specific, very recent memory shard. How should she respond to that? All she managed was, "Oh."

Hadn't she wanted this? For AL17 to remember her and pick up where she and Aiden had left off? Was that happening now? She wasn't sure how she felt about that after his initial rejection.

And she knew now that he wasn't Aiden, not really. AL17 was a different man, his genetic code be damned.

"Does it bother you?" he asked.

She hesitated. *Yes. No. Mostly yes, for reasons I couldn't explain.* "Sort of."

"Would you prefer I leave New Eden?"

She hadn't expected that. "No. Didn't we talk about this? Why would you do that? Where would you go?"

"There's always work to be found in other parts of the galaxy."

Her response was automatic. "No way. You know hardly anything about the outside galaxy."

"And you do?" There was a teasing note in his voice, the first she'd heard from him, but it was still familiar. Her heart lurched.

"I know that it's a huge place and there's almost nothing in this sector, except a waystation that takes about three days to get to. This is your home," she said, surprising herself. "Don't go. Your friends care about you."

He didn't reply immediately. When she looked at him, he had a thoughtful expression, the most human one he'd had since he'd been activated. "What about you?"

Her breath caught, heart rate picking up, slamming against her ribs. "What about me?"

"Do you care about me?"

Yes. No. Sort of. I care about you, but I don't know you and I loved your previous clone. Maybe? "Yes."

He blinked at her response, schooling his expression into something neutral, more cyborg-like. "Was that question inappropriate?"

"No."

He visibly relaxed, another reminder of Aiden. "I care about you too."

A bolt of heat shot through her at the admission, and

she couldn't decide if she should be irritated by it or not. Definitely inappropriate! Her mouth went dry, which was just as well, because she was at a loss for words.

"Have I said something wrong?"

She shook her head. "No."

His hand slipped over to hers, still clutching the journal. His skin was cool and dry, his fingertips ending with tiny ports, leftover from his time generating in the cloning tank. They lightly scraped against her skin, drawing a shudder of pleasure from her. If he noticed, he didn't let on. Her body, traitorous and confused thing it was, responded, unaware that it wasn't Aiden sitting next to her.

Or maybe he was, in a way, if Aiden's memories were returning.

The primal part of her longed to throw her arms around him and let him hold her, but she didn't know how he would respond to that. Instead, she relaxed her hand, letting his fingers fall between hers. His slowly curled around hers, the small motion making her breath hitch. So did his. She remained motionless as he leaned over her head. "You smell good," he murmured into her hair.

Goose bumps rose along her skin, which now felt too hot and tight for her body. His breath lightly ruffled her hair, his head moving lower so his lips could lightly graze her ear. The long-forgotten thrum of arousal coiled low in her belly, ready to spring at the slightest encouragement.

"Ai—" she whispered, voice hoarse, catching herself from saying Aiden's name in time.

He paused, breath still hot and steady against her skin, sending tingles skittering across it. She held hers, unsure of what he was going to do next. To her disappointment, he pulled away, releasing his hold on her hand. "My apologies," he said, his voice strained.

It took a few seconds for her brain to process what he'd said. "Why?"

He hesitated before explaining. "I'm not sure. Taking liberties?"

Taking liberties. What an old-fashioned thing to say. It was oddly charming. "You didn't." Had he? She wasn't sure. She had welcomed his touch, certainly.

He moved away from her, putting only a few centimeters' distance between them, but it felt like so much more. "I can see why he loved you so much."

She hadn't been expecting that. Shocked into silence, she couldn't form a reply. But any answer she might have had for him evaporated before she could voice it as the seismology monitoring equipment erupted into chaos, sirens wailing and panels' lights flashing red.

———

IT TOOK HALF a second for AL17 to be on his feet, calling for the rest of his cyborg brethren to come to the seismology center. *It's happening!*

Pauline screamed, the sound competing with the alarms before they shut off on their own. On impulse, he grabbed her in a hug, holding her against him as tightly as he could without hurting her. Her pulse pounded through her veins with a terrifying speed, so hard his sensors registered it. A sob escaped her, and he kissed the top of her head, hoping he could provide some measure of reassurance.

"They're off," he said. "Maybe it was a false alarm." With no small amount of reluctance, he let go of her, noting that she clung to his arm like a lifeline. Warily, he checked the readout on the nearest comp.

Tsunami pending, estimated time 50 hours, estimated .80 meter runup anticipated.

A chill slithered through him. New Eden's earthquake had been devastating. A tsunami could render the entire settlement uninhabitable. "Fuck," he said. Dimly, a voice in the back of his mind reminded him that this was the first time he'd said a swear word in front of Pauline.

"We're going to die." Pauline tightened her grip on him and burst into tears.

"No." His voice was firm, more confident than he felt.

Rhys was beside them before she could reply, Tommy and Simon at his heels. AL17 could pick up the presence of everyone else connected to their link, running to the center as fast as they could. "Impending tsunami," AL17 reported.

Rhys stood in front of another comp console, data streaming across its clearscreen too fast for an unenhanced person to read. AL17 did the same, bringing up the same information. "There's an anomaly under the water," he announced.

"I saw that. But New Eden's tectonic plates beneath the ocean haven't shifted, nor is there any impending move-ment that our equipment can't read," Rhys replied.

AL17 sneaked a glance at Pauline, who appeared puzzled. It was better than terrified. Still, his heart hurt when he saw the tear tracks on her face. "How is that possible?" she asked. "I'm hardly an expert, but don't plates have to move to cause a tsunami or an earthquake?"

"Yes." Rhys's response was grim. The rest of the cyborgs streamed into the center, eyes silvery as they filled each other in on what had just happened. "The anomaly under the water likely isn't of natural origin."

A hard, cold ball of dread lodged itself in AL17's

stomach as possibilities about whatever was under the ocean raced through his mind. "An aquatic predator?" He turned back to the comp screen, noting the anomaly Rhys had mentioned. Something small by ocean standards, spherical in a way that didn't occur outside a laboratory setting.

Or a weapons manufacturer.

"It's an explosive," AL17 announced.

"What the fuck?" muttered Simon. AL17 was inclined to agree with that assessment.

Rhys tore his gaze from the comp screen to look at everyone in turn, incredulity across his face. "How the hell was a bomb implanted under the ocean?"

AL17 immediately accessed every file he had on the New Eden settlement, information racing across his vision at a speed that had his head swimming and his body swaying a little. Other than the likelihood of New Eden being established as a criminal hideaway, he found nothing about weapons manufacturing. The planet didn't have a smithy, with anything metal-based having been brought to New Eden with the original settlers. The planet didn't even have so much as a gun anywhere. Replying to Rhys, he said, "Beats the hell out of me."

Silence fell over the room, and he had the sneaking suspicion it had nothing to do with the bomb at the bottom of the ocean. Glancing at the puzzled expressions on the faces of everyone assembled, he added, "What?"

"You sounded just like Aiden, is all," Tommy explained.

"I *am* his clone," AL17 replied, confused.

"I know, but your inflection, the look on your face..." Tommy shook his head. "Never mind, we have other shit to worry about now. How long do we have to defuse this thing?" He peered at the console readings. "Fifty hours, tops?"

Rhys shook his head. "I would prefer to assume that we don't have the luxury of fifty hours, if this is a man-made explosive. We don't know what exactly we're dealing with yet." A look of distaste crossed his features. "We'll have to go underwater to disable it."

Brandon's voice rang out from the back of the room. "You don't have to go."

Rhys's lips thinned. "I should."

"Someone who hates deep water as much as you do should stay out of it altogether. I know you want to help, but if you freeze up down there, you'd be a liability for everyone else. I'll go. It doesn't bother me much," Brandon said.

"We still have to conduct an analysis before we do that." Connor, now. Ever the pragmatic and levelheaded man.

"There's also the rest of the New Eden population to consider," said AL17, just as his sensors picked up humans running to the center. Most of the homes were now equipped with seismic equipment. They would have heard the wailing alarms. Heard them and then nearly died of fright.

"The bomb isn't showing signs of imminent detonation, but that could change at any moment," said Rhys. Before he could continue, a sobbing Hannah threw herself into his arms. He immediately responded, murmuring reassuring words into her hair. Behind her, the rest of the New Edeners, save for the still-underwater Si'laar, poured inside until the center was packed.

The Si'laar! Horrified, he checked the comp again to be doubly certain that they had only received a warning, that their undersea habitat was still undisturbed. Relief poured through him when he confirmed it. They were safe for now.

AL17 glanced at Pauline, who still looked like every

nerve in her body was on edge, waiting for something terrible to happen again. He wished he could do what Rhys was doing right now—not just for her benefit, but his too. He liked holding her. She felt familiar and safe. But he resisted the impulse, keeping his hands at his side.

"How are we going to explain this?" Simon asked, his voice barely audible over the din of terrified questions peppered at the cyborgs, at each other, to themselves. It was difficult to parse them out. Jasmine pushed her way through the crowd, Darius's hand in hers, to reach him. Simon responded as Rhys did, wrapping an arm around each.

Rhys's expression wasn't reassuring to AL17. An unfamiliar, unwelcome emotion welled in him, and it took a few seconds for him to recognize what it was. *Fear.* Fear for Pauline, for New Eden, for all of them who didn't know what to do next about the weapon under the sea that could permanently destroy the planet. Needing to touch her, he clasped Pauline's hand. She squeezed back, a gesture that chipped away at his terror, if only a little.

"I don't know," Rhys replied, surveying the crowd. "By all the gods, I don't know."

Unlike everyone else, Pauline hadn't minded community meetings that much. Before the earthquake, they'd been held in a community center—led by Rodelle Lansing's priggish husband, Jackson—short jaunts that emphasized the importance of working together to preserve limited supplies, like glassware. Since the cyborgs' arrival, they'd been held in the amphitheater, led by Hannah and Rhys. Pauline was glad to see someone else willing and able to lead their people, having never harbored any desire to be a leader herself.

But today, looking at everyone crammed into the seismology center, so many that some couldn't get in, she noted the terrified looks on everyone's faces and could tell that no one knew what to do about what was hiding beneath the surface of the water. *A bomb! What the fuck?*

Confused and frightened voices babbled around her, and a few cyborgs' eyes had gone blank, a sure sign they were speaking to each other telepathically. The memory of Aiden correcting her on that term ("My love, we aren't psychic, just technologically advanced") surfaced. "What are they saying?" she asked AL17, who still stood beside her, his hand wrapped around hers, eyes silvery and blank.

"That there wasn't anything on the clearscreens brought back from the north that included information about weaponry," he replied. His brow furrowed. "Some of us will have to go underwater to examine it and see if we can disarm it."

"And if we can't?" Panic crept into Rodelle's voice at the possibility.

"Then we'll evacuate the planet."

Her breath caught. She'd never considered such a thing, despite two starships waiting not even a kilometer away from her home. "Oh, my God."

He leaned down, his breath tickling her skin as he whispered his next words. "I promise that you will be safe from whatever happens next. You are not going to die as long as I am alive."

Heat coursed through her body, making her breath stutter. His nearness and the familiar husky whisper in her ear shouldn't be affecting her that way, especially considering the knowledge that the entire planet was in grave danger.

Before she could reply, Rhys spoke, his voice booming across the room. "There is an imminent threat to our safety via a tsunami." A few strangled sobs sounded from the crowd. "This is not a natural phenomenon but one that has been man made via an explosive device that was implanted on the ocean floor. The alert we received estimated that we have up to fifty hours before it is expected to detonate. We are working with the assumption that we have less time to find a solution to this."

"What if we don't?" The question came from Ollie West, who, in his sixties, was New Eden's oldest resident. Pauline saw Hannah instinctively flinch at the sound of his voice, no doubt waiting for a barrage of questions no one could answer yet. But Ollie's face had a pinched, worried look on it that Pauline had never seen before. He was just as scared and felt just as helpless as everyone else.

"Then we'll evacuate the planet," Rhys replied, echoing AL17's earlier assertion. "It will be a tight fit, but between our starship and the Si'laar's, we can accommodate everyone to leave New Eden."

He didn't say so, but there was an unspoken truth lingering after his statement—they might not be able to return. While knowing that they had a decent chance of survival was reassuring, the possibility of losing their home, imperfect as it may be, was heartbreaking and just as terrifying as the impending tsunami.

To Pauline's surprise, the evacuation announcement didn't rouse another round of questions or shouts. Instead, everyone was quiet, ruminating on the possibility of having to leave. Finally, Ollie asked, "Why can't you disable whatever's under there with your comp equipment?"

AL17 spoke up. "Its construction predates our equipment. Its materials are registering as a concentrated abinocrotoluene, powered by an accelerant called distorlion. Both have been banned across the galaxy, due to their instability. Some of us will have to go underwater to see if we can disable it. We can't do that remotely with its construction, and it's too old to connect with our equipment."

"You know my friends are down there, right?" The petulance Ollie was notorious for had returned to his voice, scored with an undercurrent of fear.

"Our friends will be safe. It will be prudent to ask them to return to their starship for their daytime sleep until we can determine exactly what's down there," AL17 replied.

His response was calm and smooth, without the robotic notes he had shortly after his activation.

He sounds like Aiden. Despite the seriousness of the situation, the reminder was stark. This was how Pauline imagined Aiden would have reacted during a crisis.

"Can you get Korjek and everyone out of the water now?" Ollie pleaded. "It isn't safe for them there."

Rhys's reply was surprisingly gentle. "It would be prudent to do so later tonight, when they aren't sleeping. We know it won't detonate between now and when they come out of the water."

"How can you tell it won't blow up when you can't disable it? And you said the materials were unstable. Isn't that the point of a bomb?" Ollie demanded.

"Explosive weaponry should be controllable to be effective," Rhys replied. A shadow crossed his face. No doubt, his previous iterations had been responsible for horrific things involving explosives at some point.

"There may have been a minute shift in the tectonic plates for it to alert us to its presence," AL17 added. "Nothing that would cause seismic activity in and of itself, but just enough to make its presence known." To Rhys, he added, "And to think, you considered only making the equipment responsive to strictly environmental threats."

Pauline's breath caught and held. How the hell had he known that? She hadn't been at meetings where the equipment designs were discussed, but AL17 hadn't been, either. Judging by the shocked looks on everyone around her, they'd noticed AL17's remark too. She thought she might have heard a pin drop in the seismology center at his last admonishment.

Rhys blinked, a deliberate motion that was the only indication he'd noticed something amiss in his otherwise stoic expression. "I did. I'm glad I was talked out of it."

"The New Edeners are unlikely to have planted it, anyway," Darius piped up. "There's no way abinocrotoluene or distorlion could be refined on this planet."

"Those elements were used in the construction of incendiary devices favored by a criminal empire that originated in the Milky Way system about three hundred years ago," Connor announced from the doorway. Pauline hadn't noticed him until now.

"How do you know that?" Darius asked suspiciously.

Connor gave the other cyborg a look that questioned his intelligence, then tapped his head. "You do know I can use the implants in my brain to access knowledge of the universe?"

"Yeah, it's just—you learned that really fast." Darius blushed. Simon squeezed his hand.

"It's settled, then. At some point, whoever the original New Edeners ripped off, pissed off—whatever they did— someone from the criminal syndicate arrived in secret, planted a bomb in retaliation, and it failed to go off." Connor shrugged, as if what he spoke about wasn't a matter of life or death. "The fact that the original settlers were able to survive without being killed by their criminal overlords, even without the presence of a bomb, speaks to their resilience and intelligence." Before anyone could refute that, he added, "I know their intelligence is in question, given what their actions have led to here. But there is a level of admiration necessary for these people to establish a colony on the farthest edges of the galaxy and stay alive for over a century."

"You're awfully calm about this," muttered Pauline under her breath before she could stop herself.

"Panicking accomplishes nothing," Connor retorted, undoubtedly using his cybernetically enhanced hearing to its full capacity.

Pauline didn't reply. AL17 reached for her hand and squeezed it, a gesture that was both reassuring and strangely stimulating. Once again, she was reminded of Aiden, an entirely inappropriate bolt of heat shooting through her.

"Connor's right," AL17 said. "We should stay level-headed and calm. Deactivating this thing is within our skill set."

Rhys nodded. A few other people, cybernetic and unenhanced alike, were doing the same. Now that the initial terror had passed and the immediate threat had been addressed—or, at least, mostly addressed—a sense of uneasy peace fell over everyone assembled. The seismology tech worked.

And so did the tech that stitched together AL17. Who, since this afternoon, had started developing mannerisms of, and looked and sounded just like, Aiden.

THE SUNS WERE DIPPING beneath the horizon when the crowd finally started to dissipate. A few people lingered, asking the cyborgs questions about how the seismology equipment actually worked, where they could go if they had to evacuate New Eden, if they could return if the worst happened. Pauline half listened to the chatter, distracted by AL17's confident answers, so unlike his earlier stiff demeanor. It was as if something had switched in his brain, making him more empathetic, more human. As if Aiden's personality had been transplanted into him. She knew clones tended to hang on to traits, but she was pretty sure AL17's recent shift into Aiden's mannerisms wasn't normal by their standards.

She and AL17 stayed for the rest of her shift at the

center, with Pauline watching and listening while he talked about what was under the water with a few of the other cyborgs. Her heart clenched when she thought about what lay ahead of them: working in the dark water, hoping nothing would blow up before the planet could be evacuated.

Taking a deep breath, she steeled herself. Of course, nothing bad would happen. They had a handle on things and a workable plan and backup plan.

To her surprise, AL17 walked with her out of the center. "Can I take you home?" he asked.

A thrill coursed through her, hardly the first inappropriate one she'd had today. Her answer came out breathier than she intended. "Yes."

Neither of them spoke as they walked along the overgrown path, a silence Pauline was grateful for. Confused thoughts raced through her mind—AL17's role in the bomb defusing, the possibility of evacuating the only home she'd ever known, how she'd felt when his lips hovered so close to her face before the alarm blared.

She sneaked a glance at him, noting that the hard set of his jaw was replaced with a more relaxed expression. Less determined, less mechanical, more…human.

When they reached her front door, he paused as she ascended the porch's stairs. Hand on the doorknob, she said, "Thank you for your help today."

He shrugged. "What else would I do? I care about this place."

She hesitated before speaking again, carefully parsing her words. "You remembered something that happened before you were activated. When you were talking with Rhys about the seismology tech?"

He nodded. "I realized that after I said it."

"That was kind of weird." She blurted it out before she

could stop herself. Hurt flashed across his features, and she immediately wished she could take it back. "Not a bad kind of weird. But I don't think any new iteration has remembered something like that so clearly, so soon after they were activated. I'm not upset."

"Just disturbed." There was an undercurrent of sorrow in his voice that tore at her.

"No! Surprised, is all. I've had a lot of shocks over the last couple of years." Forcing herself to smile, she added, "That wasn't a bad surprise. Just unexpected. I didn't know new iterations could recall such specific memories."

"Neither did I, nor Connor."

"You asked him?"

"He briefly mentioned it via our link after I asked Rhys. At some point, I should go to the sickbay and get checked out." He shrugged, but there was a line of worry between his brows. Whether it was because of the memory shards or her, she had no idea.

Pauline twisted the knob and pushed in the door. "I could go with you, if you want support."

The line smoothed and his face split into a grin. Her heart skipped a beat. Aiden had given her the exact same expression the first time he saw her.

"Do you want to come inside?" she asked. *Maybe something in here will jog his memory again.* A flicker of hope, that Aiden might be returning to her, flared to life again. She knew she should extinguish it, protect her heart against further devastating loss if that wasn't what was happening, but after so many years of existing and waiting for her turn to die, she needed to believe anything was possible.

He tilted his head in surprise. "Could I get a glass of water?"

"Of course." Stepping inside, she held the door for

him. It eased closed on its own behind them on creaking hinges.

She almost told him to help himself, as if he would know how everything was arranged. As it was, he surveyed the small space, filled with old furniture, threadbare home-made rugs, and the laundry Pauline hadn't bothered to put away since she last scrubbed her clothes in the kitchen sink, then haphazardly tossed in a woven basket. Aiden had noted she was messy on his first night with her. It turned out, when he wasn't confined to living in a recharging pod, he wasn't much tidier than she was.

She poured a glass of water for him from the kitchen pump, which he accepted with a shy smile. "Thank you."

"You're welcome."

He took a few swallows, then looked around the space again. "Your bedroom is upstairs to the left," he said, voice quiet. "The bed is a meter from the window, which has an old bedsheet for a curtain."

Her breath stilled, her vision swimming for a few seconds. She had hoped he would remember the house, but to have confirmation that he did... "Yes."

"I remember."

Tears pricked her eyes, and she desperately hoped he didn't notice them. Forcing them away, she said, "Are you —how do you feel about that?"

His answer was soft, wistful. "Like I know you and this house, but I don't. I'm unsure how else to describe it. I don't know what happened today, but it's like a switch was flipped, and now I know so much about Aiden, like he's part of me. He is," he corrected himself before she could reply. "But I have reason to believe that this isn't how new iterations function." His lips formed a wry smile, one she wanted to kiss. "I hope I'm not broken."

"Don't even joke about that. Do you know what happened to Rhys?"

"Vaguely. Maybe it will come back to me in a few days, or you could tell me the details."

She shuddered. "No. I only heard about what happened when his brain's hardware malfunctioned. There was a lot of blood. I hate blood."

"Even when it's a life force?"

Pauline gave him her best withering look. *It almost feels like we're getting back to normal.* "As long as blood stays where it belongs, I'm good."

"The heart." Reaching for her hand, he pressed it to his chest. Beneath his black shirt, his heart beat against her fingertips, a steady tempo that was picking up speed.

It's me. I'm the cause of that. Her heartbeat had picked up too.

It was a corny thing to say, something Aiden would have said as a joke, but it had the impact of a crashing wave against Pauline. *Bad analogy*, she reminded herself, thinking of the impending tsunami threat. Her gaze fixed on AL17's face, on the longing expression reflected there. She knew he wanted to kiss her.

He doesn't know how.

Without disentangling her hand from his, she stood on tiptoe, hoping she wasn't about to embarrass him or make a fool of herself. The memory of their encounter in the seismology center before everything went to hell, how affected they'd been by each other's nearness, returned.

It was all the encouragement he needed. Bending down, he brushed his lips against hers, hesitant at first. Heat flooded through her, the familiar thrum of arousal rushing through her veins for the first time in months, but she didn't move, not wanting to scare him.

Or start something they didn't have time to finish.

She sighed against his mouth, then kissed him again, deepening it. A moan escaped him as he responded, her name a whisper on his lips when he reluctantly pulled away.

"I have to go," he said regretfully.

She nodded. "I know."

"I'll be okay out there. I promise."

Anything could happen, either in the sickbay when he was getting checked out for hardware anomalies or when he was underwater. "I'll hold you to that," she said.

A smile bloomed on his face. Gently tracing the outline of her lips with his thumb, he said, "Pauline, I will come back in one piece this time."

CHAPTER FOURTEEN

AL17's PARTING words to Pauline rattled around his head like a stone in a jar, alternating with the memory of how it felt to kiss her. It was proving more difficult than he expected to push the thoughts away for awhile, to focus on the task at hand, which was descending seventeen meters below sea level, where the explosive device waited to be defused.

Focus. You were programmed to focus. AL17 stared ahead of him at the sea, the waves gentle in the evening darkness. Tommy stood beside him, Simon to his left. To his right was Brandon, who was coming along, despite his partner Rodelle's protests that he stay on land. Bringing up the rear was Darius, armed with a toolkit and flashlight. Noticeably absent was Rhys, who, according to Brandon, had an intense phobia of deep water.

Even though his body was designed to function underwater without the aid of a breathing apparatus, nervousness welled up in AL17 as all of them began their descent. The Si'laar's underwater habitat had been emptied, with the alien contingent spending the evening with Ollie. AL17 thought back to the older man's relief as Korjek emerged from the water earlier in the evening and the hearty clap Ollie had given them on their back when he realized his friend was safe.

It felt like everyone on New Eden had found a friend or lover or both, except AL17. Did Pauline count as a friend? He wasn't sure where they stood on that front—was his attraction one-sided? Had she kissed him out of curiosity or, worse, pity? She had loved Aiden fiercely, probably still did. A wave of jealousy for a dead man rolled through him with the same force as the sea's cold water, lapping at his knees, crawling up his thighs…

Fuck, but that's cold. As his body temperature automatically adjusted, a sigh of relief escaped him.

Brandon elbowed him in the side. "What was that for?" AL17 muttered.

The other cyborg's answer was whispered, not that it would matter, when everyone else in the water had enhanced hearing. "Focus. You're woolgathering."

"How can you tell?"

"Because I do it too."

They walked farther into the water, the gentle waves now reaching their waists.

A memory of Brandon standing over something flooded assailed AL17. He saw and heard everything clearly—bright sunshine, the rush of a nearby waterfall, a gigantic water-filled metal chasm at his booted feet next to Brandon's, mere centimeters from the edge of a platform. A roof? A dock? He couldn't tell. But he could sense RH103—Rhys—in the dark water, terror coursing through him. Beyond that, he could hear Brandon speaking to him through their shared link, reminding him that he could still breathe, that he was safe.

Brandon cares about other people. Not that the other

cyborgs didn't, but there was something unique about him. He was more in touch with his human side than the others tended to be. He was a safe person to be around, to confide in.

The water was now up to their chests, drops splashing their faces. AL17 connected to their shared link in his brain's circuitry. *Can I ask you something?*

His reply was quick. *Sure.*

I don't want to be distracted from what we have to focus on when we get down there, so I'll ask you now. AL17 hesitated before his next words, suddenly feeling a little…shy? Was that the correct word? Was he overstepping? *Your partner is Rodelle, is that right?*

Yes.

Water splashed AL17's face. Soldiering on, he kept walking, his boots' gravity function kicking in and making his feet uncomfortably heavy. In the back of his mind, a sensor reminded him that the sensation would be fleeting as his body's cybernetics adjusted. Water filled his mouth. Coughing, he resisted the urge to hold his breath as they walked under the waves while his respiratory system shifted functions. He wondered why he didn't have gills. *How did you know she was the person for you?*

Brandon sputtered as water entered his nose. *It was kind of a mutual thing. We were friends first, and things progressed from there. She let me live in her house. Most of us roomed with New Edeners. It was a way to build trust and show them that we were willing to live like they do. I just like sleeping in a bed, to be honest. Now that I've had a taste of living like a normal human, I can't go back to cruising through space. Why do you ask?*

The water was past AL17's eyes, covering his head, filling his ears. While he wasn't exactly afraid, he could see why Rhys hated deep water so much. *I don't know how to describe it,* he replied. *Pauline is very special to me. I keep looking for reasons to talk to her, I look forward to when I'll see her next, I worry about her.*

His night vision activated, as did the other cyborgs', casting eerie, otherworldly glowing through the water. AL17 sneaked a glance at Brandon, who raised a brow at him.

Did you know that Aiden and Pauline were heavy pretty quickly when we first arrived? he asked.

Yes, I've heard about that. He remembered some of it too.

Brandon took his time replying. *Well, it was love at first sight. Or lust, maybe. I don't know the specifics and I don't need to. You're probably feeling the same pull you—Aiden—did the first time.*

It didn't escape AL17's notice that Brandon stumbled over his name. *Like fate?* he asked.

If you want to think of it that way, sure. You're drawn to each other on some deep, primal instinct, at least. Aiden and Pauline adored each other from the very beginning. You—they were the first couple to hook up.

AL17 sidestepped Brandon's latest gaffe. *Hook up?*

It's an old-world term, I think. It means shacking up. Catching AL17's confused expression, Brandon sighed, exhaling bubbles. *Sleeping together. That's also a euphemism, by the way.*

A shadowy image of Pauline's naked body beneath his filled his mind. His mouth went dry, which was ridiculous, considering his surroundings. *Got it.* AL17 realized he was breathing comfortably underwater, undoubtedly due to Brandon's distracting him. *You're really good at this, you know that?*

Good at what?

Making me forget that I'm not breathing air and that my feelings for Pauline aren't totally irrational.

My original wasn't military, so I never had the emotions beaten out of me. I try to be supportive when my friends have questions about them.

AL17 hadn't had any recollections of his original yet, only that memory shard of himself dying under a blazing sun in the desert. He had no idea if that was a vision from his original or a clone, if his original had been military or not. *I'm glad you retained that.*

Well, I'm better at preparing a roast than I am taking a bomb apart, so you may want to save your accolades for when we get through this.

AL17 grinned, knowing that Brandon wouldn't have been permitted on this trip if he didn't have at least a rudimentary understanding of explosives.

The sea floor sharply slanted, his boots growing heavier again as their anti-grav function fought against nature. Pressure built up in his ears, making his head ache until his cybernetics adjusted. The sea floor's sandy bottom gave way to sharp rocks, bits of plant growth visible here and there. Not a fish was to be seen, nor any evidence of marine fauna. According to the New Eden history that had been uploaded into his brain, the oceans had been overfished, the native and introduced species long extinct.

A map of the sea floor was superimposed in his brain, a bright red dot blinking where the explosive waited. AL17's heartbeat sped up in a way that had nothing to do with the physical exertion of walking underwater, and irritatingly, his sensors did nothing to quell it. He'd promised to return to Pauline in one piece. He would make good on that vow.

The device is eight meters ahead, Darius reported. *Be careful.*

Nervousness slithered down AL17's spine as they walked closer to the red spot on the map. Quickly accessing New Eden's geologic data, scant as it was, he was only slightly reassured that the presence of five grown men was unlikely to cause further shifting of the planet's tectonic plates. Trying to take his mind off the impending danger, he wondered how deep the plates could be. As far as oceans went, this one on New Eden was fairly shallow, so the plates would be thinner than those found on other planets, so...

Here it is. Darius's voice broke through his thoughts. AL17 halted and glanced at the sea floor. Silt swirled around his boots.

Half a meter ahead of them was an innocuous-looking box. Square shaped, perhaps ten centimeters long and wide, its metal sides still shiny under their light, despite its age. It was wedged between two broken-looking pieces of sea floor that took AL17 a few seconds to recognize as tectonic plates. Bright blue-green fronds poked up between the plates, covering the box. *Could the plant life's growth be what disturbed it?* AL17 asked. *It looks new to me, not that I'm much of a judge for these things.*

Possibly, Simon piped up, speaking for the first time.

It looks like the grass native to New Eden that's outside the settlement, Brandon said. *We saw a lot of it when we went to the north. The original settlers probably clear-cut it away to plant their own grass seeds and crops. It grows quickly.*

How the hell did it end up here? Simon asked.

Darius enlarged the flashlight's beam, making the bomb appear brighter. *Weeds can be very hardy. We can conduct an analysis of another part of the sea floor some other time and see where else this weird shit is growing. There's a bomb in front of us, remember?*

AL17 nodded. *Let's get started. The sooner we defuse this thing, the sooner we can get back on land.*

That's the spirit! Darius replied.

An image of the bomb's materials appeared in AL17's mind, superimposed over the bomb. As they had theorized in the seismology center, the device was centuries old, made of long-banned unstable materials. Its exterior appeared to be an odd titanium-distorlion alloy that hadn't registered on the center's comps.

That's a strange choice for a protective shell, said Darius, echoing AL17's thoughts.

Titanium would help prevent rusting, said Brandon.

And could prevent the device from prematurely detonating. It's mixed with an accelerant, said Tommy, speaking for the first time.

AL17's anxiety gave way to relief. *The titanium could help act as a buffer. Wouldn't that make deactivating or even transporting it safer?*

It could, but we don't know for certain how this is supposed to be detonated. Its appearance, location, and materials indicate that it would have been remotely controlled. Of course, we don't have such a control, said Simon.

Darius's tone was tense, noticeable even in silence. *There wasn't anything in the data on the clearscreens brought back from the north that indicated such a controller existed.*

Clearscreens.

AL17 froze. A memory flashed before his eyes: being aboard their starship, helping to repair a fraying component in the cargo bay. A coupler, maybe? He was crawling through an access tunnel, laser splicer in hand to fix it. "We dumped the contents in the ship's comps." Darius's voice bounced down the tunnel from his spot in the cargo bay.

"What was on…" Aiden—AL16—didn't finish his sentence before electricity coursed through him, frying his circuits and stopping his heart.

Everything went black, his memory shifting into a void as Aiden instantly died.

AL17 froze for half a second as terror washed over him, then shook his head, trying to clear the memory, unable to let himself dwell on it immediately. There was time enough later to relive the terror.

Are you okay? Brandon asked him privately.

He was astute. AL17 had to give him credit for that. *Yes,* he lied.

Brandon didn't look like he believed him but didn't question AL17's answer.

Any further discussion about AL17's mental state was halted by Darius's voice. *I have a distortion deaccelerant,* he announced. *It will take three of us to apply it, so I can open the bomb's container and deactivate that. Simon, Tommy, Brandon— you'll apply it while AL17 holds the flashlight. Tommy, you'll also act as a spotter, in case something goes wrong.*

Wouldn't we all be in pieces if something goes wrong? Tommy asked.

Darius gave him a withering look. *Yes, but I have every faith that nothing will blow up tonight, even if we don't get it fully deactivated. That's what I mean by something going wrong.*

A shudder rippled through AL17. His pride was a little shaken that he would be delegated to flashlight-holder, but it was probably for the best if he was having memory shards flood his head every time he turned it.

He accepted the flashlight, watching as the others crowded around the metal box. Darius distributed deaccelerant patches to Simon, Brandon, and Tommy, then held a scanner over it, his lips pursed in concentration as the device analyzed the bomb and its container. *It's safe to apply the deaccelerant,* he announced. *The titanium really weakened it, thank all the gods.*

AL17 breathed a sigh of relief, bubbles issuing from his mouth.

With the skilled precision of a surgeon, Darius fitted a digital file into the box's seal and pried it open. Inside was a knot of hardware and gears, dotted with a few lights that blinked red at lazy, irregular intervals. AL17 held his breath, certain for a few heart-stopping seconds that they were about to be blown up.

Nothing happened, other than Darius's rapid scan of the device. *I have good news and bad news,* he said. Before anyone could ask for either, he continued. *The good news is, our initial estimate of fifty hours before detonation was correct when the alarms went off. The bad news is, this thing is now counting down, and we now have forty-four hours, tops, before it explodes and sets off a tsunami that will be large enough to level the entire settlement. The really bad news is that it was designed not to be defused. Any attempt to do so would result in an explosion.*

AL17's heart sank. His hand trembled, the flashlight's beam quivering in his hand. Poor Pauline, about to lose everything.

Should we prep for a planet-wide evacuation? Tommy asked. The defeat in his tone was palpable. So much work had gone into reviving New Eden.

An idea struck AL17, insane and probably unworkable. But he had to ask. *Can the bomb be moved and allowed to detonate elsewhere?*

Theoretically, Darius replied after a moment, as if mulling over the option in his mind. *Why?*

What if we remove it and eject it into space to explode there?

All of them stared at AL17, shocked into silence. *It's worth exploring,* he added.

Darius slowly nodded. *You know, that's crazy enough that it might work.*

CHAPTER FIFTEEN

Pauline anxiously waited at the shore, unable to quell her heart's rapid thundering against her ribs. She was a few meters away from the pebbled beach, as instructed by Rhys, who stood in ankle-deep water, trying to communicate with the others below the water's surface. With him were a few other cyborgs Pauline didn't know very well—Anthony, formerly AQ58, and Garrett, who had once been GL97—all in silent communication with each other.

Tibbot, Hannah, Rodelle, and Jasmine surrounded Pauline, all looking as nervous as she felt. Tibbot's baby occasionally made squeaking noises that sounded like a kitten's mewls, their tiny arms clinging to Tibbot's tunic. Behind them, a pile of towels waited for the cyborgs' return. From a distance, Ollie's and Korjek's voices could occasionally be heard as they chatted on Ollie's porch, undoubtedly complaining about how the bomb defusing was being handled. Pauline didn't have it in her to point it out and giggle with the others.

"Rhys really wanted to go," Hannah said quietly. "He feels like a bit of a failure for staying on land."

"He wouldn't be of much use down there if he freezes up in water," Rodelle pointed out.

"He could be cloned again," Pauline said.

The group fell silent. "You know we can talk about that," she continued. Thinking about AL17's increasingly Aiden-like behaviors and mannerisms, she added, "He's turning into Aiden."

The other women exchanged glances. Tibbot only nodded, clearly unsurprised by this turn of events. "Connor improved the cloning technique with our help. Korjek's help," they quickly amended. "It has been much advanced since the cyborg stole our tech."

The shift in conversation seemed to take all of their minds away from the bomb threat. "Connor did say something about that, but I thought it would mean a faster-growing clone or something," Pauline said.

"The physical growth is slightly increased, but the brain matter composition has been changed since the original tech's theft," Tibbot explained.

This revelation was intriguing. "They have memories of all their previous clones, don't they?" Pauline asked.

"Yes, but not the personal characteristics," Tibbot replied. Their baby squealed and raised their head from Tibbot's shoulder. The baby had recently started growing white hair to match the rest of their unit's. "The new tech, as Connor used it, could create what is considered a near-perfect copy of the previous subject, instead of a new person. Does that make sense? I believe I have translated this to the best of my ability."

Pauline was at a loss for words. Rodelle, Hannah, and Jasmine were silent too, waiting for her reaction. "That explains a couple of things," she finally said.

She had waited by AL17's tank for Aiden to be reborn, to return to her. And he may well have done so, based on their most recent interactions. But was he really Aiden or a different version of him? She thought about Aiden's grave in the cemetery, still so new that grass hadn't grown over the overturned earth. She wasn't sure how she felt about that—grieving him while he was in front of her. She wasn't sure how she felt about everything with AL17 and Aiden anymore.

Turning her gaze back to the sea, her heart twisted. He was still underwater, doing something insanely dangerous. She did care about AL17, albeit in a different way to Aiden.

He promised to come back to me. She had the notion he meant that he wouldn't be returning to her as AL18.

Five heads emerged from the sea. A frisson of desire coursed through her as she recognized AL17, water sluicing down his face. It clung to his clothes, highlighting the planes of his body under the light of the moon overhead. She couldn't see any of their faces too clearly yet, but she did notice that none of them seemed to be holding anything bomb-shaped.

She ran to the beach, the other women behind her. Tibbot lingered behind, murmuring to their baby in hushed tones. "What happened?" Pauline asked as AL17 walked ashore.

None of their eyes had gone blank or silvery, the sign of their communicating silently through their shared link. She did notice that none of them looked happy or triumphant that they'd defused a bomb. "AL17?" Pauline said, reaching for him. She put her hand on his wrist, his skin warm despite his time on the sea floor.

"We found it," he said, voice low. His tone gave nothing away, but she suspected he did not have the good news she was hoping for.

"And?" Beside her, Jasmine, Simon, and Darius were

having a joyful reunion, like they had been gone for weeks instead of a couple of hours.

AL17 nodded and pointed behind her. "Maybe we should wait until we can explain everything to everyone."

Pauline turned her head to see the rest of New Eden waiting on the edge of the settlement, as if being farther away from the ocean would protect them in the event of a tsunami. "Is it bad?" she whispered.

He leaned down, water dripping onto her bare shoulder. Despite the gravity of their situation, another shudder of pleasure rippled through her, sending her nerves on fire and desire forming a ball low in her belly. "It is, but we have an idea."

"Will we have to leave New Eden?"

"I don't know yet. We'll have to talk about what we found." He picked up his stride to rejoin the others.

"Wait. I brought a towel for you." She found the pile and picked one up, holding it out.

He halted in his steps and accepted it. Instead of running it over his face and hair, he examined it, his tense expression shifting to one of curiosity. "This is from the back of the door in your bathroom," he whispered in wonder.

Pauline wasn't so surprised to hear him say that. "Yeah, it was the one you used when we lived together."

She didn't realize her gaffe until AL17's gaze fixed on hers. Was it a gaffe? Hadn't they just talked about how AL17 was likelier to be an extension of Aiden with the newer cloning technology? Did AL17 have an inkling of what and who he was, too?

When he finally spoke, his voice was hoarse, like he was on the verge of tears. "Yes, it was."

———

ANY FURTHER DISCUSSION about AL17's memories was halted by the announcement of what had been found under the sea. Darius spoke at length about the discovery, flanked on either side by Simon and Jasmine.

"It's wedged between two tectonic plates," he explained. "It's expected that plates shift over time, and it usually happens without major seismic activity. The explosive was placed there deliberately, and after the best examination we could make underwater with the tools we have, we determined that the timer mechanism failed. It likely should have detonated shortly after it was planted, probably before or when the first settlers arrived."

"So, that means the original settlers weren't as stealthy as they thought they were when they ran away from that crime syndicate," Pauline said. All eyes turned to look at her, likely because she was usually quiet during these meetings. AL17 reached between them and squeezed her hand.

"Probably not, but we haven't found any written records from the syndicate themselves, nor plans of a surprise bomb," Darius replied.

"Of course you wouldn't. Criminals typically don't write down their plans for all the world to see," Ollie said. Beside him, Korjek let out a strange sound, covering their mouth in an attempt to muffle it. Probably a laugh. They really were Ollie's perfect Si'laar counterpart.

"You do realize that we have clearscreens loaded with information about the settlers' illegal activities? I helped haul them back here myself," Brandon said.

That reminder shut up Ollie and Korjek. They glanced at each other, and Pauline could tell they were already thinking about what to criticize when the meeting was over and they could go back to sitting on Ollie's porch, drinking dandelion tea.

"The device's original timer seems to have failed for

whatever reason," Darius continued. "It was likely set to detonate a few days or weeks after it was planted and didn't. The bomb itself isn't especially sophisticated, but its materials have degraded over the years, and it will explode within the next forty-four hours, by our estimate. Undersea movement seems to be the reason for its impending detonation, possibly caused by the recent growth of undersea flora over it, rather than plate movement."

"Have the plates moved at all?" Rodelle asked, sounding confused. Pauline didn't blame her; she was too.

"There's been no movement out of the ordinary. What alerted the seismology center comps is the device itself shifting because of the plant growth. That's what set off the alarms. There isn't an impending earthquake caused by natural means."

Darius spoke very plainly, without a trace of nervousness. Despite the grave news they were receiving, Pauline let herself relax a little. They knew what the threat was, and it seemed like they might have an idea about how to neutralize it.

"Are you going to defuse it, then?" Pauline asked.

For the first time, Darius looked a little flustered. So did Rhys. *Oh, no.* She felt herself blanch.

"We can't deactivate it," Darius said. "It has a failsafe that will result in an explosion, should an attempt be made. We may be able to safely move it, though."

Her heart sank. "Should we start preparing for an evacuation, then?"

Darius hesitated, then looked at the crowd, fixing his gaze on AL17. "Not necessarily."

Her stomach turned over. Why was he looking at AL17 like that? As the most recent clone, the most disposable, was he going to be sacrificed to get rid of this thing? "Wait a minute," she began, but stopped when AL17 squeezed her hand again.

"We may be able to remove it and let it naturally detonate in space," AL17 clarified.

Whatever Pauline had been expecting, it hadn't been that. "What the fuck?" she whispered. Judging by the looks on the faces around her, they were thinking the same thing.

"It's not a bad idea to explore," Rhys said. "The alternative is evacuating and letting a tsunami completely destroy the settlement. Rebuilding would be incredibly difficult, if not impossible."

And where would they go? Cruise deep space, picking up supplies on random stations, evading whatever unfriendlies could be out there? Pauline didn't have the urge to explore the stars like some others did. She was happy to stay in New Eden, speaking the same version of Standard she always had that was all but extinct everywhere else, content to write poems in her journal and work her shifts in the seismology center. Not to mention that almost no one in New Eden had been vaccinated against whatever weird diseases were out there. Pauline was happy to see New Eden eventually open to new residents and travelers, but she had little desire to embark on those adventures herself.

To her surprise, the murmurs of the crowd sounded like they were in favor of ejecting the bomb into space. "What is your proposal to safely conduct this endeavor?" Korjek asked.

"The most efficient way would be to transfer it to our starship, then take it off world," Rhys said. "It would be ejected from the cargo bay."

"It was AL17's idea," Darius added. "It's a good one, I think."

"Perhaps the only viable method of disposal," Korjek

said thoughtfully. Their single white brow furrowed in concentration. "Have you considered potential damage to your ship? It is not designed to accommodate such dangerous..." They fumbled for their next words, lost in translation.

Tibbot's Standard was more fluent. "Payload," they finished.

"Yes. Payload," Korjek repeated, rolling the syllables around on their tongue. "I am familiar with your vessel. It may not move at the velocity or speed necessary to escape its detonation."

"Wouldn't it need oxygen to explode?" Hannah asked. "I would expect it to just kind of poof out of existence in a giant vacuum."

"How do you know about how bombs work?" Jasmine asked.

Hannah shrugged. "It's basic chemistry and physics. I have to have a working knowledge of that for our agricenter."

Her casual dismissal of her knowledge aside, Pauline couldn't help but be impressed.

"Yes, an older explosive would require oxygen," Korjek replied.

"This *is* an old explosive," Hannah pointed out.

"No, its manufacture is rudimentary by the standards of today, but it is modern enough that it can detonate without oxygen, It is what you have called a 'fail safe,'" Korjek explained. Hannah's face fell.

"But I think you may have a good solution for this problem, aside from the limitation of your starship," Korjek continued. "There are small vessels aboard ours that may be more appropriate."

"They are escape pods!" Tibbot exclaimed. "They are not designed for bomb extraction!"

"They can be easily modified," Korjek said. Their face split into a grin, the first such expression Pauline had ever seen from the Si'laar. "Come, let us talk about this. We all have ideas, and there must be a way to make them work together."

CHAPTER SIXTEEN

Dawn was breaking when the meeting ended, New Eden's twin suns slowly rising over the sea, pink and orange streaks painting the sky. Despite the exhaustion and anxiety radiating off everyone, there was a stubborn sense of responsibility among New Edeners, Si'laar, and cyborgs alike; if they stayed awake and talked things through more, they might get closer to a confirmation that AL17's insane idea would work.

He definitely felt more confident about it after the late-night discussions. Korjek was certain an escape pod from the Si'laar ship would be perfect for launching the bomb off-world, and the more AL17 thought about it, the more he was convinced too.

His internal chronometer told him it was half past five when Rhys broke up the meeting, all but ordering everyone to get some rest. AL17 didn't argue. He was running on auxiliary power, in need of some proper downtime. And Pauline looked like she was about to drop to the ground. As it was, she swayed on her feet when she finally turned around and started walking to their house.

Her house. The reminder was harsh, but necessary. It hadn't been his, but hers and Aiden's. Even though he was increasingly feeling like the dead man, assuming his memories and finding himself drawn to the woman he had adored, he was still fresh out of a cloning tank, another person altogether. Wasn't he?

He watched her walk away, her gait lurching a little as it did when she was tired. She always felt stiff when exhaustion set in, he remembered, and started to follow her. Just to be certain that she was all right, he told himself.

"Hey," he said when he reached her.

She looked up, the rising suns catching the highlights in her blonde hair, the strands lightly frizzing around her face like a halo. Her eyes were shadowed, but she still gave him a smile that made his breath catch. "Hi." She played with a loose thread on the towel over her shoulder, the one she had saved for him when he got out of the water. "Thank you for saving New Eden."

His heart swelled at the praise. "I haven't done it yet."

"You have a great idea that's going to save us all." She took a deep breath, then tried not to yawn.

He refrained from pointing out that they had less than two days to put his plan into action, and there were still so many things that could go wrong. "I hope so."

She raised an eyebrow. "I know so."

He didn't reply, instead studying her face, memorizing it. He knew what her skin felt like under his fingers, even though he had hardly touched her. Knew it and wanted to confirm. But he kept his hands tightly clenched at his sides. She didn't break eye contact. Maybe she was doing the same thing.

"Where are you going now?" she asked.

Was it his imagination, or was there a husky note in her

voice that hadn't been there before? "I need some rest. I thought I would go to the ship and recharge in a pod."

Her eyes widened in surprise. "Did you want to come back to my house?" Her question came out in a rush.

Joy surged through him at the invitation. His response was immediate. "Yes."

She smiled. "Good." Just as quickly, it faded. "I'm not expecting anything," she continued. Color touched her cheeks, spreading to the tips of her ears. It was adorable.

"I'm not, either," he replied. He reached out, tucking a strand of hair behind her ear. She leaned into his touch, closing her eyes. "I just—I want to be with you." He swallowed, unsure how his next words would be construed but needing to tell her, anyway. "I know why he did too."

Jealousy flared in him, the emotion unexpected and unwelcome, when he thought about Aiden and Pauline. It was completely irrational. He was grown from Aiden's DNA; the dead man was a part of him, yet he couldn't tamp it down. He hoped it didn't show on his face.

She closed her eyes, and he was fairly certain she was fighting tears and not knowing why they were there. He understood that. He'd experienced something similar when he got out of the water and saw her waiting for him. A feeling that was too big for his body, too big to contain, that he didn't have a name for yet. A need to be with her.

A couple of tears leaked from the corners of her eyes. When she spoke, her voice was hoarse. "Come home with me."

He nodded, then laced his fingers through hers. Part of him wanted to pick her up bodily and carry her home—it was something Aiden used to do—but he didn't know how she would react to that. Baby steps, he reminded himself.

She leaned against him as they walked, her shoulder against his arm, her exhaustion and stress palpable, even through his layers of clothes. When they reached the house, she held open the door for him. "I'm glad you're okay."

He stepped through the threshold. "I promised I'd come back in one piece."

"I know, but I worried a lot." Closing the door behind them, she gave him a tired smile. "Do you want to take a bath? I can't imagine you feel that clean after being on the seafloor for so long."

"The water here isn't terribly polluted," he pointed out. "And if it was, my cybernetics have ways to filter out anything bad."

"The offer's open."

A memory of Aiden and Pauline in a warm spring together suddenly surfaced. It was early evening, in a secluded area near the power station. Their clothes were bunched up on a pebbled shore a few meters away while they frolicked together in the water. Heat roiled through his body at the sight of her, wet and shining in the light of the setting sun.

Somehow, he knew she wasn't offering to join him in the bathtub. "I think I'd like that," he said. He looked at the stairs, covered with an old carpet runner, its color long faded to mottled gray. He could picture the bathroom perfectly, with its hand pump in the metal sink, the old commode with a wall-mounted tank, the scratched tub, the floor covered in cracked reddish-orange tiles. "Is the shower function still broken?"

She blinked in surprise. "Yes."

Of course, it would be. Who else would fix it? Aiden had said he would look into that the day before he died, then promptly forgot about it. AL17 swallowed. "I see." He plucked the towel off Pauline's shoulder and turned away, putting his hand on the stairs' old banister.

"AL17."

He paused, then looked over his shoulder at Pauline, her back still to the door. "Yes?"

"Make yourself comfortable," she said softly. Something in him unfurled and relaxed. She wasn't upset or put off by his memory shards. "Do you want me to leave some blankets on the couch, or are you going to get some sleep in bed?"

There was only one bed in this house. A little too small for both of them, but Pauline used to joke that it just meant they were cozier. Aiden had loved it, loved her nearness while they slept.

"I'll be joining you," he said.

She smiled, then crossed the short distance to the stairs. "Good. I'll wait up for you."

PAULINE LAY IN BED, her earlier exhaustion pushed aside as she listened for AL17. The memory of their chat about the bathroom's broken shower function rolled over in her mind, along with when she had talked about it last with Aiden before he died. Part of her wanted to banish the memory altogether, to remind herself that Aiden may well have returned to her as she'd originally longed for. He had, in a way. Just not as she'd expected when she kept up her vigil outside his cloning tank. He was Aiden, yet wasn't.

The suns were peeking around the makeshift curtain when he padded into the bedroom barefoot, rays winking off the hardware in his body, which was covered by only a towel wrapped around his waist. Her breath caught, and a frisson of desire shot through her at the sight. She sat up, leaning against the pillows. "You have more metal," she blurted.

AL17 stopped in his tracks and looked down at his chest. There were more ports under his collarbone than Aiden had, and ones in his arms were smaller. The metal was shinier, much newer, maybe a Si'laar-devised alloy that improved on the cyborgs' tech. Dimly, Tibbot's explanation for AL17's uncanny resemblance to Aiden rang through her mind. What if AL17 wasn't so much a clone as a reincarnation of his previous iteration?

"This contains access to my cybernetic enhancements and implants," he explained, puzzled.

"I know. There's just more of it than there used to be." She paused, unsure how he wanted to navigate this conversation. "Does it bother you to talk about this?"

He stripped off his towel. Holding her breath, she wasn't sure if she was relieved or disappointed to see he was wearing underwear. "Just leave it draped over the door," she said, when he looked around to see what to do with the towel. He did so, just as Aiden used to.

"No. I think this is something we need to talk about," he said. He hesitated, looking at the bed. She shifted over as best she could and patted the space next to her, still holding an indentation from Aiden's body.

He slid in under the sheet, giving her a shy smile as he did so. Now it was her turn to hesitate. Should she cuddle up with him, given the lack of space?

AL17 wrapped an arm around her, drawing her to his chest. "Come here."

She was glad to do so, obediently laying her head on him. "Thank you."

He traced light circles on her bare shoulder, a familiar, comforting gesture. "What for?"

She fumbled with her words, wanting to get the right ones out the first time. "For following your instincts."

He barked out a short laugh, the first she'd heard from him since he came out of the tank. "I didn't for a while."

"You did, when memories started returning. And that was what I wanted originally. I missed Aiden so much, and then when you were activated and weren't exactly like him, I was as devastated as I'd been when they told me he had died. No," she suddenly said, needing to correct herself. "It was a different kind of grief."

"Like he had died all over again?"

"Yes, but it was the death of my dreams and hopes, you know? We had talked about starting a family after rebuilding the house, doing normal people stuff."

He tightened his hold around her. "I feel like him," he admitted. "I don't know how to explain it. I've had memories of earlier iterations, but the ones from Aiden are the strongest. And Aiden's memories don't feel like someone else's memories, the way our flashbacks do, but that I've actually lived them. I can remember their context, and if I think about it, I remember more than just bits and pieces of someone else's life. I feel like I was a blank slate coming out of the cloning tank, but after a few days, it's like I picked up where Aiden left off. A slate is like a chalkboard, I think," he explained.

"Why are you telling me about slates when you've just dropped this bombshell on me?" She cringed. "Sorry, bad choice of words."

"Because you were going to ask what a slate is."

"I was not, because you told me about them when we first met and I asked you about your cloning experience, and that's how you described activation as AL16."

You told me about them. Not *Aiden* told me about them. Her words hung in the air, but whether they were an accusation or confirmation of what they both suspected—that

AL17 was Aiden or somehow becoming him—she couldn't tell.

For a moment, the only sound in the room was that of their breathing, soft and steady. She wondered what he was thinking.

"I did tell you," he finally said. "It was the morning after our first night together, after our ship landed. I slept in here."

Her heart beat so hard against her rib cage that she was certain he could hear it. Arousal at the memory of that first night pulsed through her, amplified by the knowledge that AL17 remembered it now. "We didn't do much sleeping."

His voice was rough. "I wanted to know everything about you. I wanted you to know everything about me. The others—when I said I needed to see you after I was activated and started getting memories—said we were the first couple here, that we were drawn to each other."

"Magnets," Pauline said softly.

"Yeah, like magnets. Which one of us said that?"

"Probably me. That's about as far as my scientific knowledge goes."

"My point is, I wanted you immediately. I still do. It's unreasonable to be jealous of a dead man, but I am, even though I have his memories."

She squeezed her eyes shut to keep an unexpected wave of tears from falling. How long had she waited to hear something like that? "Aren't you him?" she couldn't help but ask.

"I feel like I am. Can you call me Aiden, or do you think I should pick out another name?"

"Yes," she said.

"Yes to what?"

"Yes to being Aiden." Despite her best efforts, a sniffle

escaped her. "If you feel like you're him and you have his memories, and you…" She nearly said "love me," but stopped herself. She wasn't sure they were there yet. Eventually, she told herself. "If you're him, you should use his name. Your name."

His breath came heavier, and she realized he was fighting tears too. "I think I am."

With that, he tilted her chin up to meet his face and kissed her.

CHAPTER SEVENTEEN

PAULINE TREMBLED AGAINST HIM, the thin material of her short nightgown hardly a barrier between their bodies. He was acutely aware of her nearness, with every nerve in his body on high alert, his cock hard against his thigh as she snuggled closer against his chest, like she was afraid he would disappear if she let go.

He had promised her he would return in one piece, and he meant it. He always would. Even if he was the one who would end up taking the bomb off-world, he would return to her without being cloned again.

He kissed her back, shifting so he could better reach her, his hands roving over her body. The planes of her were familiar to him, yet the sensations his sensors registered were new to his body. Her hand trailed along his chest, pausing over the small square metal plate implanted in his breastbone. A shudder of pleasure rippled through him as his sensors registered her fingertips, imprinting them on his memory as clearly as if she had touched his skin. She pulled away long enough to say, "This wasn't here before."

"Hearts are delicate things. I'll engrave your name on it after we get through this."

"So everyone knows you're mine." She pressed her ear to his chest, as if listening for a heartbeat. "Is it weird that we're just lazing in bed while the rest of the planet is freaking out?"

"I don't hear any screams."

"Oh, my God, you know what I mean." Tilting her head, she looked up at him, dark eyes searching his face. "Doesn't it feel, I don't know, decadent and selfish to be in bed while there's a fucking bomb under the ocean?"

"Technically, it's between two tectonic plates and visible on the seafloor, so it's in the ocean." Catching her withering look, he added, "I know what you mean. And it does feel decadent and selfish to be doing this, but no one is going to be of any use to safely dispose of that if we don't get rest."

"You could recharge faster in one of the pods," Pauline suggested.

He raised an eyebrow. "Are you trying to get rid of me?"

"Of course not. I'm thinking about the rest of New Eden. And besides, if we're annihilated by a tsunami, we'll never get the chance to see how our story plays out. I want you to be well-rested for it and for us." Her eyes fell to half-mast, a sign of her arousal he'd forgotten until now.

His heart skipped a beat at her reply. *Our story*. He remembered writing a note to her on lumpy paper that had been re-pulped so much it turned gray, his pencil catching on the bumps. He didn't remember the words he'd written, only that they were full of love for her.

He stilled for a second as the realization and memory hit him. He'd joked about how it had been love at first sight with her, how he'd seen Pauline lingering at the back of the crowd assembled at the amphitheater the night the cyborg contingent landed. How her dark gaze fixed on him, a knowing look, full of trust he hadn't yet earned that made his breath stutter and touched his soul. He'd never considered himself to have one until then.

"I want that too," he replied.

"To not die in a tsunami or make up for lost time in bed?"

"Both." There was something else he needed to ask her, before they progressed any further. "Would it bother you if I used the name Aiden?"

She blinked in surprise. "No. Why would it?"

"Because he's dead and buried in the cemetery?" It was discomfiting to him to think about his previous iteration that way.

Pauline hesitated before replying. "You know, I've hardly even been there since he—since you died."

"Really?"

"Yeah, I spent most of my time beside your tank, talking to you, telling you how much I missed you and loved you, talking about our future. That's why it was so devastating when you woke up and didn't know who I was."

His breath hitched at the mention of love, and with it, hope flared in him that she might feel the same for his current iteration. She'd mentioned it in the past tense, and it was probably too early in this relationship to ask if she felt the same. He would be satisfied with what she offered him now and would ask for no more.

I love her. I think I always have. It was why he'd been drawn to her, had sought her out. First, it was from a place of curiosity and strange familiarity, then as his memories returned, powerful need.

He responded by kissing her deeply, his tongue sweeping past her lips to claim her mouth. Her low moan of desire sent heat roiling through him, his circuitry warring with his emotions, setting off internal alarms that warned him about his increased heart rate and blood flow diverting to… He grinned against her mouth.

Pauline lifted her head. "What is it?"

"You'd never believe me."

She arched an eyebrow, still managing to make it look no-nonsense, even though her eyes were glazed over with lust. Sheepishly, he admitted, "My brain comp just told me that there's an alarming increase in blood flow to my penis and suggests that I run a self-diagnostic."

Pauline snorted, then buried her face in his shoulder to muffle her laughter. "I'm sure we can do something about that without running to the sickbay."

A dozen erotic scenarios came to mind, silencing any mirth he might have had. He thought his mouth went dry, but when Pauline kissed him again, it felt as it should—hot, wet, needy for her. Despite his eagerness and an erection that was now so hard it was painful, a ribbon of doubt unspooled in him. Something must have changed in his expression, because Pauline asked gently, "Hey, is everything all right?" She touched his hair, too short to brush back from his forehead in a way that he remembered her doing with his previous iteration.

He nodded and swallowed. "Just a little nervous, is all. I haven't been intimate with anyone yet."

Pauline's reply was soft, understanding. "It's okay. We were each other's first and onlys. We made it work then, and we'll make it work now."

That was news to him. "What?"

"You didn't know?"

"No. I suppose I haven't thought about it until now." None of his memory shards featured any woman but Pauline, which, in retrospect, made sense. Everyone he'd spoken to about his dead iteration emphasized the instant connection between them before anything else.

"We figured everything out pretty quickly," she said. "Although I should tell you we had a lot of practice." Her smile was wry and knowing, a look reserved only for him. She dusted his jaw with light kisses, the small touches nearly enough to set his nerve endings on fire, and it took everything in him to maintain his control. Even so, he reached under the sheet to stroke his cock, to take some of the edge off his arousal. It did nothing.

Pauline watched as he did so, her hand following his to mimic his actions. A groan of pleasure escaped him, his body bucking against the mattress. If she kept that up… "Pauline." It felt amazing, an awakening of sensation that he could only have imagined until now. Yet he wanted to experience as much as he could with her this morning, and that wouldn't happen if she didn't stop.

She must have recognized something about the urgency in his voice because she removed her hand. "Yes?"

He immediately regretted it but knew it had to be done. "I—I'm not going to last very long if you keep that up."

"It's been a while, hasn't it?" She raised herself from the mattress enough to strip off her thin nightgown, revealing her bare body to him.

Sucking in a gasp of surprise, he reached out to touch one of her perfect breasts, the skin soft beneath his fingertips. A shudder of pleasure coursed through her, and her eyes closed in response. As he rolled her nipple between his fingers, she muffled a harsh cry, teeth biting her lower lip. Encouraged, he switched to her other breast, then leaned forward, taking her nipple into his mouth.

Her hand reached for his hair, gripping it. "Aiden," she gasped.

Hearing his name on her lips nearly made him come on the sheet. A small voice reminded him that she probably wouldn't mind, that she would say something about all the reasons to try again, but he still wanted to do everything he could with her before the planet-saving task ahead. He needed this with her, this chance to rekindle the physical connection he'd been craving since…

Since I heard her when I was in the tank.

He released her nipple and urged her back down to the mattress until her head lay against the pillow. There was one thing he wanted to do to her before he fucked her, something that he now remembered he'd immediately enjoyed. He pushed the sheet aside and kissed a trail down her body, his eyes on her chest to watch its rapid rise and fall. She raised her head, eyes locking with his, hers half-hooded with desire as she realized what he was going to do. "Yes," she breathed.

Her legs had fallen open, revealing her glistening sex, wet and waiting for him.

An unexpected wave of confidence surged in him as he kissed her, tongue experimentally swiping her folds. Her body jerked against him, a cry escaping her, mingled with a breathy, "Aiden!"

Hearing her use his name was all the encouragement he needed. He would never tire of her saying it, knowing he was hers in this life and beyond. He doubled his efforts, relying on instinct and her body's reactions until her legs began to shake on either side of his head and a wail was drawn from her throat as she climaxed against his face.

He pressed a kiss to her thigh, then raised his head. She had levered herself up on her elbows to better see him. Her cheeks were flushed, eyes still glazed with desire, mouth a round O of surprise. "You're really good at that."

Pride coursed through him at that pronouncement.

"Will I have the chance to practice, so I can get better at it?"

She gave him a look that clearly questioned his intelligence. He grinned in response.

He shifted so he was positioned over her, gently kissing her neck. "How do you want to do this?" he murmured against her skin.

Her reply came out in a hoarse whisper. "After all the time, I'm not fussy, as long as it gets done."

So bossy. He liked it. Taking his cock in hand, he guided it to her entrance, shaking his head when she reached for it. "If you touch it, it'll be over before it starts."

He sank into her, forcing himself to maintain control, her wet heat overwhelming. She took a few deep breaths as he did, and he moved as slowly as he could, not wanting to hurt her. When he was fully seated inside her, he pressed his forehead to hers, tears unexpectedly coming to his eyes. *I love her so much.*

Pauline's hips lifted and her legs wrapped him, urging him on. With a silent prayer of thanks to the universe, he thrust into her, the sound of her low moans increasing with his tempo. Her body began to quiver in time with his as he felt his orgasm build, and with her name on his lips, he exploded, collapsing against her, then rolling both of them on their sides, hearts thundering in tandem.

———

HE WOKE UP WITH A START, his internal chronometer telling him he had been lightly sleeping for twenty-one minutes. Pauline lay beside him on her side, her head cradled by a pillow that was long overdue to be replaced. Taking care not to wake her, Aiden slid out of bed and retrieved the sheet that had fallen to the floor, gently draping it over her. She murmured something unintelligible in her sleep but didn't wake.

Despite his imminent need for more rest, he knew he wouldn't be able to sleep. Not until he had some answers about who and what he was, and his memory banks didn't have that data accessible to him. He needed to speak to Connor, needed to find out exactly what had been done to him during the cloning process. By all accounts, his experience wasn't typical.

Not that I'm complaining. But it was still puzzling, and he wanted to ensure that it wasn't dangerous.

He picked up his clothes from the night before, noting that they smelled like seawater. Wrinkling his nose, he tossed them back to the floor and hoped Pauline wouldn't mind. He vaguely remembered both of them talking about taking up better housekeeping habits, so maybe she wouldn't. Glancing around the bedroom, he honed in on a wooden dresser, the middle drawer crooked and sagging. Something told him that the drawer would fall out altogether if he touched it, so he gingerly opened the bottom one with a faint rusty squeak, finding an assortment of handmade garments. He lifted out a tunic that was too large to be Pauline's.

These were Aiden's clothes. He remembered taking them down from a washing line and folding them the day he died. A chill coursed through him at the memory.

He sneaked a glance at Pauline, still asleep. She had saved everything in case he came back, leaving it just as he'd left it. He dug out underwear—cyborg issue, he noted —and a pair of shorts, taking care when he closed the drawer to keep it from making noise. With his clothes in hand, he went to the bathroom to wash up.

When his boots were on his feet and he was ready to leave the house, he hesitated before opening the door.

What if Pauline woke up before he returned? "A note," he murmured. "We always left notes for each other."

There was usually a box with recycled paper and pencils in the living room. Ducking into it, he spotted it on a low table, on top of the journal she had been writing in when the alarms blared at the seismology center. Part of him wanted to see what she had written, but he resisted the temptation to open it and instead flipped open the box lid.

It was already filled with notes, written in a hand that he instinctively recognized as his. He picked up a few and leafed through them to find words of love for her, along with observations, doodles of a pair of smiling suns, poorly drawn stick figures of the two of them. There were notes from her to him, little poems and drawings better than anything he could create.

The tears that had threatened him when he was making love to her returned. He had something precious with Pauline, before he'd died and now.

Gathering himself, he found a clean piece of paper in the bottom of the box. Spying a pen next to the journal, he wrote, *Gone to the hospital to get checked out.* Would that make her panic? He added, *Nothing serious. I'll be back soon.*

Should he write "I love you"? Probably not, since he hadn't said it aloud yet. Instead, he signed it with a heart, then left it in the middle of the table.

He walked into bright sunshine, deceptively cheerful, considering the threat that lay under the sea. Letting himself into the small hospital, he found Connor in an examination room, sending Ollie West on his way. "You are fit for space travel," Connor said, sounding as if he had repeated himself multiple times. "You will not die aboard a starship, should we need to evacuate, I promise."

Ollie did a double take when he saw Aiden in the doorway. "You're wearing his clothes," the older man said by way of greeting.

"What else should I wear?"

Ollie considered that for a second. "Point taken. Maybe we can build a shopping promenade if we live through this." To Connor, he said, "Thank you for trying your best."

Connor gave him a tight smile. "Always a pleasure."

Aiden waited until Ollie had left the hospital before speaking. "There's something I have to talk to you about."

"Of course, otherwise you wouldn't be here." Connor cast a critical eye over Aiden's apparel. "You really do look like him."

"I was cloned from his DNA. And that's why I'm here. The last day and a half—I feel like him. I don't feel like AL17 or a new person." Steeling himself, he continued. "I remember my life with Pauline, I remember the day I died, and I'm sure memories of the terraformed asteroid we had to leave will return soon."

Connor's brows lifted in surprise. "It's common to experience flashbacks, but this sounds very specific."

Aiden sat on the edge of a bed, clasping his hands in front of him. "Am I going to die again?"

"Not that I can tell, unless the planet decides to evict us more forcefully than it's already tried."

"The bomb isn't natural," Aiden said, but Connor held up a hand, silencing him.

"I know, I was making an attempt at a tasteless joke. I followed the same cloning procedure we have always used, save for a few pieces of programming from the Si'laar that they have refined over the years. We talked about this, how you're closer to a reincarnation of Aiden than a whole new clone." He gave a half shrug, as if Aiden's very existence didn't hang in the balance. "I said earlier that we would have to adopt a wait-and-see attitude about this development. It appears that our earlier suspicions were correct."

"Incredible," Aiden said.

"It's the most logical explanation. Korjek explained it to me when they helped me with the cloning programming. It has been enhanced to facilitate an easier, more precise cloning process when they combine their DNA for new Si'laar babies. I do not think you are ill or at risk of health issues. You're a near-perfect copy of Aiden Lewis, rather than a mix of the previous sixteen clones. Of course, this introduces a whole new ethics issue about what to do after one of us dies," Connor continued. "For instance, should we merely continue to clone ourselves, or is there a point when one would wish to rest for eternity? I find peace in knowing that, one day, I could live forever among the stars, but I do enjoy my time with other people. I…"

"Connor." Aiden could not handle thinking about his mortality in a spiritual way at this point.

"Understood. If you want my opinion, you are a healthy cloned male who is going to help out with the disposal of the explosive under the ocean. You should get some more sleep."

Aiden refrained from pointing out that the bomb was technically wedged between tectonic plates and not under the ocean. "So should you."

"I was on my way to do that when I left the ship and Ollie asked me about space travel, should we need to evacuate. I have every intention of going home and getting some proper rest."

"What were you doing aboard the ship?"

"I was cloning crabs." Connor sounded like he couldn't believe he was being asked that, like cloning bivalve marine creatures was a normal occurrence.

"Why?"

"For James. He's very fond of bivalves, and I've found myself developing a taste for them too."

"Got it." He hopped off the bed. "Thank you for putting my mind at ease."

"Do not forget about the bomb extraction."

Aiden sighed. "And there it goes."

CHAPTER EIGHTEEN

Sunlight streamed in through the bedsheet curtain, landing squarely on Pauline's eyes. She winced and rolled over to block it out. It had to be past noon.

Aiden was gone, but she heard shuffling downstairs. She grinned, remembering their early morning encounter, then stretched, noting that she was sore in places that hadn't been sore in a long time. Shucking off the sheet, she grabbed a tatty old robe hanging over the bedpost and slipped it on, tying its mismatched belt around her waist.

She found him in the living room, the box of love notes in his hands, poring over the months of correspondence between her and his dead clone. *He didn't die*, she reminded herself. *Not really. My God, he's wearing Aiden's clothes!* All he needed to do was grow his hair a little longer, and he would be as if his sixteenth iteration had never been killed. She froze.

He rose when he saw her, a soft look crossing his features. "Good afternoon, Pauline."

Shaking her head a little, she replied, "Hi. Sorry, I was just kind of surprised to see you there."

"I got up a little while ago and spoke to Connor. I left you a note, but you were still sleeping when I came home."

Her heart flip-flopped. "Is everything okay?"

"It seems to be, but I think I'm an anomaly so far. You were right about Connor using improved cloning tech when I was in the tank. I don't seem to be a clone of the original AL but of AL16. More of a reincarnation."

Pauline squeezed herself on the small couch between him and its arm. "But that isn't a bad sign or anything, like when Rhys had his brain fail?"

"No, I don't think so. Just a new and improved version of Aiden Lewis." He wrapped an arm around her and pressed a kiss to her temple. It was an innocent gesture, but it still sent a squad of butterflies racing through her. She leaned into him. "I've been reading these."

She nodded. "We like to pass notes."

"I remember a bunch of them. Not much of a poet, am I?"

"Of course you were. It comes from the heart, and yours were definitely heartfelt."

He groaned, prompting a smile from her.

"I didn't read your journal," he said, nodding at the notebook Jasmine had given her.

"You can if you want. There's nothing bad or especially private in there. Just stuff about how much I missed you and complaining about New Eden. I should probably add to it, let any reader know about its possible destruction." She sighed. Some of her terror about the impending bomb extraction had ebbed. The cyborgs seemed to know what they were doing, which was more than the New Edeners did, and they had a back-up plan if the settlement couldn't be saved.

Still, the idea that after everything they had accomplished together might have been for nothing rankled her, as she was sure it did everyone else. Even Ollie West seemed to be happy lately, after his lifetime of misery.

"You could write the history of New Eden for the galaxy to learn about," he suggested. "It's not like the criminals the original settlers ripped off can come back."

"Unless they're cloned," she pointed out, thinking about the recent revelation that some of the cyborgs' previous iterations had had a business relationship with the first settlers.

"Unlikely, if they haven't returned. And even if they were, aren't we proof enough that people can change?"

"Yeah." Aiden's previous iteration had told her what he recalled of his original's life. He'd worked as a pilot prior to being recruited to the brutal cyborg experiment, where he continued flying, but that was all he remembered. That, and his real name.

He wrapped an arm around her, bringing her against him. Pressing a kiss to the top of her head, he said, "I've been thinking about how to proceed with this, and it would be best if I recharged in a pod aboard the ship before tonight."

She shifted, raising her head to look at him. "Why can't you rest here?"

"Because I can do that more efficiently aboard the ship and download flight schematics from the main databanks while I'm in downtime."

It took a few seconds for the full import of his words to hit her. Outrage and hurt colored her words. "Why would you need that? You're not volunteering to pitch that thing into space yourself, are you?"

He appeared surprised at her outburst. "Of course, I'm considering it. Why wouldn't I? I have muscle memory of flying a ship and smaller craft. I can brush up on the theory while I'm resting."

"You literally just died and were resurrected! No," said Pauline, shaking her head. She stood up and paced the small space of the living room. "No, you aren't volunteering to blow yourself up. I won't allow it." Through her anger and fear that he was even considering such a thing, she felt a sliver of ridiculousness. She couldn't stand in Aiden's way if he wanted to explode. Angry, fearful tears filled her eyes. Brushing them away impatiently, she whirled around to face him. He wore an expression of shock, like he couldn't believe she wouldn't want him to put himself in harm's way to save the planet. Forcing herself to keep her voice calm, she added, "I've already lost you once. I can't handle losing you again."

"But I can be cloned again," he pointed out.

"So, that means you can put yourself in harm's way every time something terrible is about to happen? You aren't disposable. None of us are."

"I know I'm not. But I do have the skills to do this." There was an edge to his voice that told her he brooked no argument. Pauline had heard it before when he was debating with Ollie about repairs to the power station when the cyborgs first arrived.

She hated that he was probably right. Scrubbing her damp eyes with her fingertips, she asked, "Aren't there any other fighter pilots who can do this?"

"Not with my exact skill set, but I won't be going up there alone. I feel like I need to go, you know?" The look on his face was thoughtful. "I remembered two things when I came out of the tank. The first was that I'm a fighter pilot. A part of me will always belong in cockpits. The second was you. And I realize that isn't the ideal order for me to remember important things, but it's what happened."

Shame twinged through Pauline at his admission. She

did understand the pull of needing to do something for her others, even though she hadn't done that much of it lately, preferring to while away her time outside Aiden's cloning tank. She also knew that she wouldn't win an argument to keep Aiden planetside. He, just as his previous iteration, was stubborn. And if he had the ability to fly an explosive off the planet as safely as possible, he should give it a shot. "Okay," she said.

"Okay, you'll support me in this?"

Nodding, she said, "Yes."

His expression softened. "Come here."

She was only too happy to oblige, needing the contact. Pulling her into his lap, he wrapped his arms around her. "I promise I will come back in one piece, just like I came back from the water," he said.

"I don't think I can handle losing you again." Her voice broke.

"You won't. And if something goes wrong, I can be reassembled back into one piece."

"Aiden!"

"Let me have a little dark humor about this."

Leaning against his shoulder, she sighed into his shirt. "I'm just scared. For you, for all of us."

"Everyone is. But we know what's happening and how to fix it. New Eden is going to be all right."

"I hope." Her answer came out sounding more bleak than she intended, but she couldn't help it. Part of her was convinced that the worst would happen, that New Eden's short string of good luck would end.

Aiden shifted, then raised her chin in his hand so he could meet her eyes. Despite the anxiety swirling around her brain about what lay ahead, desire coursed through her. His metallic pupils dilated, a very human response, and she knew hers had to be doing the same. Her skin prickled, goose bumps popping up along her arms as she remembered how they couldn't keep their hands off each other earlier in the morning. The heavy thrum of arousal beat a steady rhythm through her, pulsing between her legs. Her earlier shock and anger at his decision to fly the bomb off-world ebbed away, replaced by desire and the need to have him inside her as soon as possible. His expression, coupled with the hard bar of his erection under her, told her he felt the same way. His eyes were heavy-lidded, glazed with lust. Whenever he looked at her like that, she felt like the most beautiful woman in the galaxy. Breath catching, she kissed him.

His response was swift. His tongue swept into her mouth, claiming her in a way that sucked away what little remained of the air in her lungs. Recovering a second later, she quickly adjusted so she was straddling his lap, his cock between her legs a pleasant and maddening pressure.

Now it was Aiden's turn to have his breath stutter, for his body to flex against her. "I really have to recharge aboard the ship," he said, voice strained, but he didn't sound convinced.

"We can wait until later," Pauline replied breathily.

His eyes darkened. "Oh, no. We're not waiting. We're going to do this, and I'm going to think about it before I fall asleep and have the sum knowledge of cyborg history dumped into my brain comp." He reached for her robe, pulling the sides apart to bare her body to his heated gaze. When he pressed a kiss to her collarbone, she shivered in tandem with his ragged breaths. The notion that this would be quick and hard flitted through her mind, sending another shudder of pleasure through her.

He noticed her reaction. "What is it?" he asked roughly.

A wry smile crept across her face. "I'm just thinking

about how much I'm enjoying discovering all of this with you again."

His hips bucked, drawing a sharp gasp from her. "Me too."

"Can we do this here, or do you want to go back to bed?" Even as he said the words, he was pulling at her robe, untying the belt's loose knot. Pauline's hands scrabbled for his shorts, and a few awkward seconds passed as he helped her shuck his clothes.

Her mouth went dry at the sight and feel of his naked body against hers. As she adjusted so she was straddling him again, her slick pussy brushed against his thigh. Aiden's eyes squeezed shut for a few seconds and he grunted in response. She didn't want to wait. She didn't know if she could wait, or if he could. "Here."

"Thank God." His body was already thrusting upward again, the movement a teasing imitation of what both of them wanted. Holding her breath in anticipation, Pauline grasped his cock, hard and hot in her hand, stroking it until he thrust again.

"Please." His whispered plea was hoarse.

"Please what?" She was enjoying this, having a little bit of power over him.

"Please, get on."

"I thought you wanted to get off?" She couldn't help but snicker at the bad joke. She would give in soon; she was dying to ride him. This morning hadn't been enough.

"I think both of us do." Without waiting for her to argue with him, he grabbed her face between his hands and kissed her, their breaths coming hard and ragged.

He was right, and she didn't want to wait anymore. She was still careful when she lowered herself onto him, guiding his cock inside her, mindful of the effects their earlier love-making still had on her. Slowly, she slid down, taking her time until he was fully seated in her. Neither of them moved as she took a moment to adjust, although Aiden's muscles tensed beneath her as he struggled to control himself.

Pauline wiggled her hips a little, the motion sending ripples of pleasure down her spine. Sliding her hands around his shoulders, she lifted herself up, then slid back down, throwing back her head as she repeated it, encouraging him to move with her.

He hardly needed any. Gripping her hips, he raised her higher, his body moving beneath hers, a fine sheen of sweat already appearing on his skin. Her name was on his lips as he thrust into her over and over, his hand sliding between their bodies to her clit, pressing his thumb to it with just enough pressure to set every nerve ending in her body on fire.

He remembered that. The realization that he did only brought her closer to an orgasm. "More." She could barely get the word out.

Aiden added a little more pressure. Between that and the heavy-lidded look of lust on his face as he watched her, it was almost enough to push her over the edge. He was holding back, judging by his controlled movements, his flushed skin. He'd done that before too, not wanting to hurt her. "It's okay." She could hardly get the words out. "You won't break me."

Her permission unleashed something in him, something primal that she'd always loved. He gripped her hip with one hand, his body sliding in and out of her in a familiar rhythm that Pauline suspected wasn't fully human. And she loved it.

She came with a shout that might have been heard across the settlement, crying out his name. A moment later, he followed, body stiffening and tensing beneath hers as his orgasm tore through him. He held her against his chest, his cock still inside her as he slowed down, wrapping his arms around her, pressing her face into his neck. "I love you," he said, his voice a warm vibration.

She raised her head. She'd been waiting to hear those words for months, but actually hearing them again nearly brought her to tears. This would be the worst possible time to cry. "You do?"

His lips greedily found hers, the kiss sending another wave of heat through her. "Yes. Like nothing else I've ever found in this life or before."

"I love you too." Her heartbeat had started to go back to its normal speed and was picking up again at their admissions. This time, she couldn't blink away her tears. "I always have. I always will."

"Which is good, because you're never getting rid of me after I send that bomb outside the atmosphere." There was a cocky grin on his face, the first time she'd seen this particular one since he was activated.

"I never want to get rid of you."

"It'll be impossible." He kissed her again, then both of them disentangled from each other. She was already missing his body inside hers when he rose. Naked, he padded into the kitchen. "Want some water?"

"That would be great, thank you." She leaned back against the couch cushions. At least it was covered by a blanket, although it had been dislodged. She made a mental note to wash it the next time she did laundry. Her house still didn't have laundry machines, like the new ones did, so she did hers in the bathtub or kitchen sink.

The sink's water pump squeaked as Aiden maneuvered its handle. He returned to the living room with a cup of water, passing it to her before settling back on the couch.

"I'll have to go back to the ship soon," he said apologetically.

She nodded, knowing he had to and hating it. "Yeah." She took a deep swallow of water, then handed the cup to Aiden, who did the same.

"It will all be okay."

She hoped so, but she still didn't have to like that he was putting himself in danger. "I know."

"You'll be at the launch?" His voice was hopeful.

"I can't believe you have to ask. Of course, I'm going to be there. I might even join you on the ship." At his sharp gasp, she added, "I'm serious. If the Si'laar's cloning techniques are so advanced that you were basically reincarnated, I'll go too."

She didn't know until the words escaped her that she wanted to go. *I'm not sure I do,* she mentally corrected herself. Pauline wanted to go with Aiden, and in a small way, help save New Eden. Other people had done that, having taken trips to waystations, traveled to the north, even built a fucking intergalactic transmitter, for God's sake, and she had merely benefited from their work. It was time that she did something, too.

Aiden was silent for a moment. Would he argue with her?

"I'm pretty sure I'll be flying in a modified Si'laar pod. There won't be room for more than one person," he said finally.

That revelation left her feeling more disappointed than she expected. "Damn."

"All I want you to do is wait for me," he said.

It sounded too simple, but judging by his earnest expression, she knew that was what he wanted. "I will."

He slid his arm around her and pressed a kiss to the top of her head. "Thank you."

CHAPTER NINETEEN

As MUCH AS Aiden hated to leave Pauline, he knew it was a necessity if this mission was going to be successful. He left her in bed after drawing a promise from her to get some rest before the extraction later in the evening.

Despite the danger that lay ahead of them, his heart sang as he strode aboard the starship. *She loves me!* Spending the rest of the day plugged into a charging pod, instead of a comfortable bed with her draped over him, would be tolerable now that she had said the words. He stepped into one that had once been the domain of the previous Aiden and connected wires into his wrist and chest ports. Leaning back against the wall, cables plugged into his body's ports, he wondered why the hell they hadn't bothered to devise this kind of thing in proper beds. There was a whole section of the ship devoted to beds, relics from before the ship had been stolen from the Si'laar. Their water-dwelling neighbors must have had them for visiting diplomats or something, given their needs.

He felt himself starting to nod off when he heard the cadence of boots clomping down the corridor. Without opening his eyes or using the cyborgs' shared link, he tried to guess who it was.

What are you doing here? Connor asked. *I would ask if you're still awake, but I can tell that you are.*

You got me. I can get better quality rest in one of these things, considering the circumstances.

Are you certain you will be able to fly out tonight? Connor sounded unusually hesitant. He stepped into another pod. There was a rustle of fabric as he pushed aside sleeves and rearranged his clothing to connect cables into his ports.

Yes. I won't be alone, anyway.

I was not referring to the presence of others in whatever stars-forsaken fighter pods the Si'laar have invented.

I was the best pilot in our group. I should be out there. The vague memory of himself behind the controls of a small fighter ship appeared. Flames were visible through the forward viewport, the dangerous sight a sharp contrast to the glee that coursed through whichever iteration of Aiden dove into a firefight.

He shuddered, pushing away the visual.

Is everything all right? Connor asked.

Other than, I can't rest if someone is speaking to me?

I see you've regained your sense of humor.

Despite his need for silence and rest, Aiden grinned. *Among other things.*

I don't need the specifics, unless it's related to your biological or cybernetic components. A suspicious note crept into Connor's tone. *Is there anything I should be concerned about on either of those fronts?*

No, unless you think that a newly hatched cyborg shouldn't be vaulted into space right away.

Our previous iterations did those things with less time out of the tank than you, so no, I'm not. Not too much, anyway. Connor hesitated for a moment. *Well, I suppose I should be, but considering the circumstances, I'm willing to let these matters slide for now.*

I'm hooked up to the ship's comp. As soon as I'm out for a rest cycle, I have every intention of uploading everything in its banks to my brain, just to be sure.

Take care not to overwrite your existing files.

Aiden rolled his eyes. *Give me a little credit. Avoiding that is as natural as breathing.* He forced himself to relax against the wall. An electrical hum filled his head as he integrated his cybernetics with the ship's comp. His backwash surge protection automatically kicked into gear, the first time it had happened since he was activated. He felt it physically, as acutely as if someone smacked him upside the head. A wave of nausea crested over him at the impact, and he was quickly flattened by his cybernetics.

At least I won't be electrocuted while I give myself a remedial crash course on everything. He took a couple of deep breaths as information began to flow through him at an inhuman speed. Some of it was familiar—the dossiers of his fellow cyborgs, including one on his most recently deceased iteration, the ship's schematics and flight logs, details about their terraformation of an asteroid, lost in the wreckage of an ion storm. Details about escape pods and shuttles that had once accompanied their starship, the crafts long lost. Dimly, Aiden thought it might be practical to look into constructing some replicas for faster jaunts to the nearest waystation.

Some unfamiliar information appeared, their code a couple of centuries old, the language long abandoned by the rest of the galaxy. Aiden stilled the information flow before he could fully fall asleep and parse through it when he woke up. It hadn't come from the starship, but was added later.

The trip to the north. This had to be on the clearscreens

Rodelle, Brandon, Connor, and James brought back with them. Aiden hadn't had an opportunity to go over it himself, his previous iteration having been killed shortly after their return.

Killed by an electrical short, too powerful for his surge protection. Surge protection he was currently relying on while he was connected to the ship. He searched the ship's memory banks for details about the previous Aiden, uploading his dossier into his brain comp. There was nothing in there that he didn't already know, if not remembered, aside from a short paragraph about his death in the access tunnel. The dead Aiden's programming and DNA were included in the file, and he ran a quick comparison between his and the dead man's.

The DNA was identical, of course. Aiden hadn't expected there to be any differences. The cybernetic components were much the same, except for the brain comp's drive, the schematics of which definitely seemed to be more advanced, thanks to the Si'laar. It was as if the brain comp and its files had been copied from his previous iteration, then prepped for implantation when his body was cloned. Aiden wasn't a clone of his original, with the memories of subsequent clones; he was a direct clone of AL16. He'd picked up his life where the dead man's had left off.

Focus. He was supposed to be focusing on training for his upcoming mission. He shunted away the DNA and cloning data, then accessed everything he could on the starship's defenses. They were familiar in an oddly comforting way, like he had come across a family scrap-book and was losing himself in the memories.

There was an unfamiliar drive in the ship's memory banks that didn't correspond to anything in his. Opening it, old code flowed through his mind, a language he didn't immediately recognize. It took a few moments for his systems to translate it to something more modern, then another spell to make it readable.

It wasn't until his body was fully asleep and power flowed through him that his brain comp downloaded the translated file and absorbed it. When the data compilation was complete, his comp lazily scanned it, looking for… Aiden wasn't sure what he was looking for.

He zeroed in on a locked file that had never been opened. He easily descrambled it, the lock being decades out of date. Lines of code that referred to the sea on the western side of the settlement. It didn't originate from New Eden, but a nearby waystation that didn't correspond to any location on the myriad star charts that were stored in his brain. The lack of a waystation wasn't the issue; those kinds of structures were decommissioned and dismantled all the time.

Appended to the ocean reference were coordinates that pointed out the exact spot where the bomb rested.

His heartbeat picked up speed. A minor alarm internally sounded, suggesting that he disconnect himself from the pod and wake up for a trip to the sickbay. Ignoring it, he scanned over the rest of the code, easily decrypting it.

Information flowed through him: details about the bomb, its construction, the materials used. The materials weren't a surprise to Aiden, given that they were easily identified by the ship's comps. What did surprise him was that the bomb manufacturer was included—an arms company that was long defunct, its lethal products no longer produced. A company that had worked closely with the military outfit that spearheaded the original cyborg project.

———

THE SUNS WERE STILL BLAZING OVERHEAD when Pauline awoke alone in bed, but she knew by their position that they would soon dip beneath the horizon. A frisson of fear snaked through her as she surveyed her bedroom from under the thin sheet. She had packed a bag in case New Eden had to evacuate, and it waited in the middle of the bedroom floor. Inside the old, fraying straw tote were charcoal portraits of her parents, drawn when she was a girl, a tarnished silver chain that belonged to one of her settler ancestors, changes of clothes for her and Aiden, and the box of their letters. The journal from Jasmine rested on top. The bag looked out of place in her bedroom, a stark reminder that nothing was normal, might never be normal again.

She quickly washed up and dressed, then headed over to the starship. Spotting Ollie sitting on his porch, she offered a wave to be polite. "You think they're gonna pull it off?" he called to her.

Pauline shrugged, the casual gesture belying anxiety that had knotted itself in her stomach. "Sure hope so."

"You headed to the ship?"

She nodded.

"Can you see if Korjek and everyone is awake yet?"

"I think they're aboard their own ship."

"You think they'd be put out if I went over to check on them?"

Something in her warmed at Ollie's concern. The man had never given a shit for anyone in Pauline's lifetime, and it was almost endearing to see him so concerned about the Si'laar. "You're friends with Korjek, right? I doubt they'd mind, as long as you don't touch anything."

Ollie nodded. "You have a point. I'll wait a bit until I'm sure I won't wake them up. Let me know if we have any bad news coming."

"Will do."

The rest of the settlement was quiet, aside from some livestock noises as she passed the agri-center. Would the animals be evacuated with them? She hoped so. They were mostly clones, but as all of them knew by now, clones weren't that different from beings produced the traditional way. She felt an odd pang of grief for the cows that might have to be left behind.

The ship's exterior door was open when she arrived, its ramp extended. Letting herself in, she blinked in the airlock, trying to get her eyes adjusted to the dimmer light inside. "Hello?"

Aiden quickly appeared, wearing little else but a pair of trousers, his bare feet slapping on the floor as he ran toward her. Wrapping her in a hug, he kissed the top of her head. "Aiden?" she said against his chest. "Is everything okay?" Quickly realizing what a stupid question that was, she amended it. "Is everything less okay than usual?"

"I'm not sure," he replied. "We're probably going to have to have a meeting, and I know how everyone hates that." Pulling away from her enough so he could better look in her eyes, he said, "But I think I know where the bomb came from."

CHAPTER TWENTY

Aiden had awoken with what felt like the sum of knowledge of the universe uploaded into his brain. He physically felt heavier, even though his cybernetics told him he was almost half a kilogram lighter after his recharge. Sticking his head out of the pod, he spotted Connor across the corridor, closed eyelids twitching before they opened and spotted Aiden. "Good sleep?" he asked, voice scratchy.

How could Connor be so casual after what had just been revealed to them? "Did you receive the download?" Aiden asked excitedly.

Connor looked at him like he had lost his mind. "What download? I'm not Darius. I'm not in the habit of acquiring raunchy cartoon broadcasts while I rest."

Aiden sidestepped the remark about Darius. Confused, he asked, "Everything on the clearscreens brought from the north?"

Connor sighed. "I don't have a clue as to what you're talking about."

"Everything from the clearscreens that was dumped into the ship's memory banks?"

"I slept upright and am feeling highly energized, albeit with a distinct lack of clearscreen knowledge, other than the bits I picked up after we returned from the north." Connor stepped out of the pod. "Are you ready for the bomb extraction? I suppose one can never really be ready, but…"

Aiden felt like grabbing his shoulders and shaking him. "Everything on the ship, everything on the clearscreens, is in my head. All the data is organized and makes sense. And it seems we have a connection to the bomb."

Connor froze mid-step, his brow furrowing. "The fuck?"

Finally, Aiden was getting through to him. "Nothing on the clearscreens has been organized. Everything seems to have just been uploaded into our banks and left as is."

Connor nodded, although the line between his eyebrows didn't smooth. "Much of the accessible data related to trading by the original settlers. And we know that some of our previous iterations conducted business with them, exchanging off-world goods for fresh water."

Aiden knew that too. "There was a lot of encrypted shit and outdated code we didn't have keys for aboard, as well. I was able to decode it."

Connor stared at him in disbelief. "You were?"

"You seem surprised."

"You were a fighter pilot. We know your original's formal education likely stopped at learning how to point and shoot."

"I'll be offended about that later. Anyway, my ability to deal with that is probably *your* doing, since you oversaw my cloning with the updated Si'laar tech. Look, the settlers' criminal syndicate seems to have been in touch with the military operation that recruited our originals for the cyborg program. They caught wind of later clones just doing their own thing, cruising through space, and must have planted the bomb with the syndicate's help to blow the entire planet out of the galaxy."

Connor didn't seem convinced. "Why would that data be on a clearscreen abandoned in the north?"

"There were pieces of transmission code that correspond to New Eden's comms tower, so transmissions between the criminal syndicate and military would have picked it up. It was encrypted, and New Eden has never had the key, so they wouldn't have been able to unpack the communication between the two. It was stored on the clearscreen, as was everything else the settlers kept records of, then abandoned and forgotten about in the north."

"This is insane," Connor muttered. He stepped back into his pod.

"What are you doing?"

"Downloading everything in those clearscreens into my head."

"It would be easier if I transferred the data to you. Mine's organized. You'll be here for hours, unpacking everything, otherwise."

"That works for me." With a sigh, he pinched the bridge of his nose between his fingers. Aiden couldn't tell if he was exhausted or frustrated. Probably both. "Send it over."

Aiden did so, the motion more difficult than he anticipated. When the data had been uploaded, he watched as Connor's eyes turned silvery, a sign the other cyborg had received the information. They stayed like that for a few minutes as he scanned it. "Huh," Connor said after a beat.

"Do you believe me now?"

"I didn't disbelieve you before, but the point stands. The original settlers really saved all the evidence, no matter what, didn't they?" Without waiting for an answer, Connor added, "They must have assumed they'd be able to decrypt that transmission at a later date, then forgot about it when they moved everything to the north before they thought they would leave."

That bit of news took Aiden by surprise. "What?"

"I found some memos that alluded to an eventual mass evacuation, drive G, section nine. Take a look."

Aiden did so, taking a few minutes to find the file. Just as Connor had said, there was a short note with the comms tower's origin code. *Cannot leave planet due to insufficient transportation and need to stay hidden; will stay here, self-sufficiency.* It was abrupt, the code broken, as if it had been corrupted. It likely had been, due to the clearscreens' age. But it was enough information to explain why New Eden had ended up as it did.

"They were eventually going to leave," he said aloud. Connor nodded. "And when they couldn't, that's when they decided to really lean into their isolation."

"That note was written a couple of years after New Eden was established," Connor replied. "What likely happened is the settlers intended to lie low for a few years, set up a working colony here, and work with the locals at nearby waystations for supplies. When they realized there was no part of the universe they could run away from, they decided to stay and told their descendants it was because they wanted to get away from technology."

"Then the original syndicate returns, plants a bomb in retaliation, fucks off, and the bomb doesn't detonate," Aiden finished. "I just don't understand why they wouldn't drop it directly on the settlement." Seeing Connor's incredulous look, he quickly added, "I'm glad they didn't. I just don't get why."

"We'll have to bounce some ideas off each other at the

next meeting," Connor replied. Tilting his head, he said, "I think we have company."

It was Pauline. Aiden didn't have to check the ship's comp to know. Without another word to Connor, he took off down the corridor, needing to see her again.

―――――

FOR THE SECOND time in Pauline's memory, New Eden was silent during a meeting. The first time it had happened was the night the cyborgs landed, and the silence had been brief while they explained who they were, why they had arrived, and why they wanted to stay. Now, Aiden held the rapt attention of everyone assembled.

The bomb had been planted in a deliberate move against New Eden and an earlier cyborg contingent, in a botched mass-murder attempt. Or maybe it was meant to be merely a massive disruption; Aiden wasn't certain as he explained what he had found in the clearscreens' files while he recharged.

"The clearscreens' data didn't only include details about trades and shady business practices," he said. "The comms tower had an invasive program that intercepted messages between ships that flew a little too close to New Eden for their liking, and occasionally, waystations. There were more of them when the planet was originally settled, although they're all gone now, of course. There wasn't incentive for permanent space settlements in this part of the galaxy at that time."

"The comms tower," said Ollie from somewhere in the back of the crowd, breaking their silence. From her vantage point beside the stage, Pauline silently agreed. "You said they intercepted data?"

Beside Aiden, Connor spoke up. "Probably looking for signs of the syndicate."

"And when they appeared, they didn't have the means to decrypt the threats," Aiden replied.

"How would they get a bomb into the ocean without anyone noticing?" Hannah, standing beside Pauline, finally spoke. "Clearly, the original settlers were monitoring for signs of life. They would have noticed if something broke atmosphere, if not for the noise. We've all heard your ship. It's *loud*."

"The comms tower's atmospheric sensors weren't as extensive as they are now," Aiden replied. "If a small-enough craft broke atmosphere far enough away from the comms tower, they likely wouldn't have noticed. And that kind of weapon can be programmed with coordinates to travel on its own to a predetermined destination after being dropped from the sky. It probably wasn't left there by a human or other sentient creature. It could have been dropped off in the north and sped here on its own with an anti-grav function to lodge itself between tectonic plates in the ocean without a single special operative or intergalactic gangster to risk themselves. In fact, I can't see any other way it *would* have been planted. If a person had planted it, it would have detonated when it was supposed to. It went where it was supposed to, something got knocked loose that prevented it from exploding, and now its components are corroded from being in the water, making it a hazard."

In Pauline's admittedly uneducated opinion, *anything* explosive in the ocean was a hazard, whether or not a component had failed. A knot of anxiety lodged itself into the pit of Pauline's stomach. While it was a weird sort of relief to know more about New Eden's true origins, part of her wanted to wait to hear about them until after the explosive in the ocean was safely taken care of.

Rhys stood between Aiden and Connor, having been quiet while the two of them spoke to the crowd. Pauline didn't know if he'd had everything from Aiden's head downloaded into his; if he hadn't, he probably would soon. As if Rhys could read the mood of everyone assembled—he likely could, with his social skills vastly improving over the last few months—he said, "This new information doesn't change our plans for the bomb's removal. We will make an attempt tonight, as we already discussed, with contingency plans for a mass evacuation if the plan fails."

A chill slithered down Pauline's spine at his last sentence. She thought about her packed bag, filled with clothes and tchotchkes of her life and Aiden's. The thought of leaving New Eden and starting over on a new planet was terrifying.

Not as terrifying as losing Aiden again. She glanced at him on the stage and saw his gaze was fixed on her. Some of her tension dissipated. As long as they were together, she could do anything.

"We're going to ask everyone to board one of the starships before we start the extraction," Rhys said. Pauline straightened a little at that announcement, noticing that everyone else seemed to, as well. "The Si'laar's ship is equipped with three small shuttles that we will use to dispose of the bomb. Aiden has agreed to pilot one." Rhys's expression darkened a little at that announcement. Pauline had been expecting that, knowing about Aiden's previous flight experience. Rhys continued, "Darius will pilot the second and Korjek the third."

"What?" Ollie's shout was louder than ever. "Who agreed to that?"

"Korjek volunteered," Rhys replied curtly. "They're a very skilled pilot."

"Why the hell—" Ollie's voice broke. When Pauline

turned to look at him, she saw Ollie's face buried in his hands, shoulders shaking with grief. Pauline's heart gave a painful squeeze at the sight. He was a blustering, angry man, but she understood why now. He'd been lonely for so many years, and now that he had a close friend, he had to stand back and watch them put themself in mortal danger.

The Si'laar contingent was now making their way to the amphitheater, roused from their daytime sleep aboard their ship. As if Korjek could sense Ollie's distress, Korjek shuffled over to where he and James stood, placing their left scaled hands on his back in a very human-like way of reassurance.

Aiden hopped off the edge of the stage, a concerned look on his face. "I know you're not okay with my decision to help with the bomb disposal," he said quietly.

"I am," she said. He didn't look convinced. "I mean, I'm not *okay* with a bomb existing, but I get why you need to do it," she quickly amended. She reached for his hands, threading her fingers through his.

"Thank you for understanding."

She nodded. The anxiety hadn't left her yet, and she hoped it didn't show on her face. "Of course."

"We're going to get started in less than an hour," he said. "Promise you'll be waiting for me at the comms tower?"

"You sound so sure that we aren't going to have to evacuate."

He shook his head. A small, knowing smile appeared on his face that made her want to kiss him. "No fucking way. We're going to get this right the first time."

CHAPTER TWENTY-ONE

THE SI'LAAR SHIP WAS DAMP. The humidity hit Aiden as soon as he boarded it, but it was missing the heat he had grown used to on New Eden. Combined with a chill that was closer to the temperature of the ocean, the interior had goose bumps popping up along his skin.

He followed Korjek and Tibbot through the bowels of the ship to a bay on its lowest deck. Tibbot's baby cooed from their sling, strapped to their chest. In the dim light, Aiden thought the baby's scales looked a little less green, shifting to a golden color that resembled their family unit's. Despite the tension and uncertainty of what lay ahead, Tibbot offered everyone a smile over their shoulder. "I do not expect you to fail. You must be there when my baby's name is chosen," they said.

"The name," Korjek began. They were silenced with a sharp look from Tibbot. Aiden vaguely remembered that Tibbot had different ideas about parenting than the rest of their family, some of which had been met with resistance from Korjek, the oldest member. Aiden was curious about the baby's name and how it would be picked, but he hadn't had a chance to research it further.

The bay held three pods, larger than Aiden expected. A memory of an escape in such a vessel appeared—he saw himself crawling into one, joking with a black-uniformed figure about how it was a little too cozy for his liking, but it would do in a pinch. Judging by the tone of his voice and the lack of urgency, he must not have been preparing to be launched into a firefight. A small measure of relief trickled through him. At least it wasn't a bad memory.

Korjek pressed a button on the top of one of the pods. "It is a standard unit," they reported. "It will respond to your commands with your..." They waved their hands under their voluminous robe.

"Hands," Darius replied from behind him. Aiden jumped, having forgotten the other cyborg was there.

Korjek nodded. "It will respond to Si'laar and human hands."

Aiden stuck his head in the open pod. Its small command console was lit up in a riot of green and yellow colors, the equipment familiar to him. It resembled a scaled-down version of the cyborgs' starship's bridge, something his previous iteration had flown more than a few times.

Darius touched his elbow. "Are you sure you want to do this? Rhys volunteered if you can't go," he murmured.

Aiden shook his head. "I'll have to be cloned again if something happens to Rhys, because Hannah will kill me."

Tibbot let out a strange sound that resembled laughter at Aiden's reply. Korjek narrowed their eyes. "This is not a time for humor."

"Gallows humor, surely," Darius added.

Korjek turned their gaze to him, their expression as close to irritated as Aiden had ever seen it. Darius's eyes widened a little and he took a step back. Tibbot shook their head, the ghost of a smile still playing on their lips.

"You may inter—" Korjek began. They paused, as if parsing for their next words. The Si'laar had worn translation devices for their first few days on New Eden, only recently acquiring enough of the planet's obsolete Standard dialect to effectively communicate. Korjek's fluency wasn't quite what Tibbot's was. Trying again, Korjek said, "You may interface with the pod directly." They tapped their head with their primary set of hands. "Your mind?"

"We can do that already aboard our ship," Darius said.

"Then this will not be strange for you," Korjek replied. "The crafts will acknowledge enhanced humanoid brains. You will look into its—its lock. Look into its lock, and the pod will respond to your commands and offer communication to the other pods." They slapped the top of the pod. "This pod is the only pod that has the tools to extract the bomb. We did not have enough to add to the other pods. You must be careful."

Aiden could handle that. *Just like I can handle hauling a bomb out of an ocean.* "I will be."

"Get in the pod and connect to it," Korjek commanded. Their voice brooked no argument.

Aiden did so. Immediately, a thin green beam of light projected from its forward viewport, zoning in on his right eye and holding. A second later, images of the pod and its functions filled his mind, every feature making itself known to him, every function available. He suspected he could probably fly the thing without the aid of his hands if he really wanted to. Just to be certain, he placed them on the command console, pleased to find out it responded to him, anyway.

"There is a modified tractor function on the underside of the pod," Korjek said. "Visualize it."

While Aiden was used to being in tune with the starship and in the heads of his cyborg brethren, actually controlling a craft by thinking about it was a novel concept, so out of pocket that he could hardly believe it was possible. But he did as Korjek asked, bringing up an image of the tractor beam beneath the pod. The device responded, activating with a jolt that had him shifting in his seat. Its schematics filled his head, a short list of abilities and restrictions. The tractor was fairly weak, only able to move something weighing less than two hundred kilograms, but it had enough power to remove an explosive.

"Huh," he said aloud. Being in the pod, being connected to it, made it feel as if electricity surged through his body. An uneasy sensation crawled through him as he remembered the last time that had happened, nearly breaking his concentration. Taking a deep breath to steady his thundering heart, he blinked, looking outside the pod's hatch at Darius, the person closest to him. He had a worried, pinched look on his face. *Are you going to be okay?* he asked through their link.

Yes. It was just a little overwhelming being connected to the pod, is all.

Darius's brows knit together, his lips turned down in a frown of disapproval. *I can handle the extraction if you're not up to it. No judgment here if you aren't.*

I've handled extractions before. I'm the same person I was before the accident. I still know how to fly something with high stakes. Aiden placed his hands on the console. The weird surge of feelings and memories in him aside, it felt good to be back on a bridge, even if it was a tiny one-person pod. It provided a sense of belonging, second only to being with Pauline. He was doing this for her.

"Do you have programmed coordinates of the device?" Korjek asked. If they or Tibbot had noticed the telltale silvery hue the cyborgs' eyes took on when they spoke over their shared link, they didn't let on.

Aiden shook his head a little, as if the motion would clear it. "Yeah." He had the exact spot of the bomb memorized, a location he now entered into the pod's comp.

Korjek nodded, then turned their sharp gaze to Darius. "You?"

"Got it."

"You have got what?"

"The plan, the gist of flying a pod." Darius tapped his head. "It's all here."

Korjek's response was crisp, almost irritated at Darius's flippant reply. "Check your pod to ensure it is there too."

"They know what they are doing," Tibbot interjected.

"It's fine," Darius said. "I get it. They want the equipment returned in one piece, your underwater home to stay intact, and New Eden to go back to its version of normal." To Korjek, he said, "Right?"

"Yes. My priorities are in a different order," Korjek replied. They inclined their head at the pod assigned to Darius. "It is almost time to begin."

PAULINE FELT like a terrible person as she held back Hannah's hair, but helping her through nausea was a distraction from everything happening outside.

They were crammed into a small white-walled lavatory in one of the guest quarters aboard the cyborgs' ship. Through the doorway, she could see her packed tote on the floor, open and spilling the contents of her life across the carpet. Aiden's clothes were tangled with hers, the box of their letters on its side. She ignored it and returned her gaze to the back of Hannah's head over the toilet. Dry heaving, she shook off Pauline, then sat on the floor, pale and shaking. "We better not evacuate," she said. "I don't think I'll be able to handle a space flight right now."

"What brought this on?" They had boarded the craft in anticipation of an emergency evacuation, then Hannah slipped away and bolted down the first corridor she found, hand over her mouth.

Hannah shook her head. "There's some weird smell in the air. Can't you tell?"

"It just smells kind of stale to me. I'm used to it." Pauline hardly noticed it, having spent so much time aboard the ship while Aiden was cloned. The ship had a dusty quality to it, mixed with something that reminded Pauline of a snuffed candle. "Are you really all right? You didn't answer my question. You don't usually get sick like this."

Hannah hesitated. Her voice was quiet when she replied. "Can you keep it to yourself if I tell you?"

Alarm flared through Pauline. "Yeah. What's wrong?"

Hannah's words came out in a rush. "I'm pregnant."

"What?" Pauline yelped. Her earlier concern gave way to a curious mix of excitement and envy. Lowering her tone to a stage whisper, she asked, "Are you sure?"

"Connor confirmed it a few days ago, although Rhys's sensors already picked up changes to my physiology before he did. We were going to start telling people a couple of days ago, but we haven't, for obvious reasons." Hannah's gaze turned beseeching. "Please don't tell anyone."

"Of course, I won't. Congratulations," Pauline whispered.

"Thank you, I think. Pregnancy kind of sucks so far. I never noticed how terrible everything smells and tastes before I got pregnant." Hannah placed a protective hand on her belly. With a scowl, she adjusted her clothing. "My shorts are getting small. I'm going to have to figure something out for clothes soon."

Pauline had started outgrowing her clothing recently, but that was due to having regular meals for the first time in years. "Do you want some help getting up?"

Hannah shook her head. "I won't need that for a few months yet. I think I'm good." Just as the words left her mouth, she covered it. Hauling herself to a kneeling position, she slammed the lavatory bathroom closed, leaving Pauline in the suite. The sound of her vomiting was louder than Pauline expected.

Hannah emerged a few moments later, still pale but looking less shaky than she had before. Before Pauline could ask if she was all right, Rhys burst into the quarters, alarm across his features. "Hannah?"

"I'm fine. Your ship absolutely reeks like something burning, by the way."

"Why didn't you call me?" he asked.

"We talked about this. I don't get to decide when I have to puke. I was trying to make sure I didn't do it all over the deck." Hannah took a couple of deep breaths. "I just need some water. And I told Pauline about our news. She won't say anything."

"I can get some water," Pauline offered.

"There are replicators in the lounge," Rhys said.

"I know. Congratulations, by the way. Your secret is safe with me."

"Thank you," Hannah said to Pauline. To Rhys, she said, "You should get back to the bridge."

"When I checked on your whereabouts with the comp, it said you were in here, and I..." Rhys's expression darkened.

"If I was really sick, I would have gone to the sickbay. I ran for the nearest toilet, which happened to be here."

Pauline felt like an interloper listening to their conversation. Slipping out of the room, she strode through the corridor, her footsteps muffled by the carpet underfoot, until she returned to the part of the ship regularly used by the cyborgs. She filled a tall mug with water from the replicator in the lounge, nodding at a few New Edeners who had gathered there. Worry had their faces drawn. A collection of bags, not unlike her tote, was stacked against a wall.

It felt like they were waiting on news of a gravely ill loved one. The memory of Aiden's death returned, of the hope that had coursed through her before Connor delivered the horrifying news that he had died. She had clung to it for as long as she could, needing to believe that he would be all right for the sake of her sanity.

But this wasn't like Aiden's death. It was closer to Rhys's accident, when news of his emergency surgery spread through the settlement like an out-of-control fire. Everyone had waited for news, unsure how the situation would go. They'd had no prior experience of such an incident, just as they didn't have any now, with the threat of a tsunami.

At least we have a chance of survival, even if New Eden might not. The thought bolstered Pauline's spirits a little.

Before she left the lounge, Jasmine grabbed her arm. "Is Hannah okay?" she asked. "She just took off and you went after her."

"She's fine." While Jasmine probably knew about Hannah's pregnancy, given how close they were, she didn't want to assume.

"Where is she?"

"One of the guest quarters."

"Are you going back there?" Jasmine asked, eyeing the cup in Pauline's hand.

She nodded.

"I'll go with you." Turning back into the corridor, Jasmine sighed. "Sorry, I have a lot on my mind, and if I stay in the lounge, I might lose it. Darius is out there."

Pauline nodded.

"Simon's working in the comms tower, helping to monitor everything, and I can't exactly bother him right now. We're both worried sick. You know what that's like."

"I do." Impulsively, Pauline grabbed Jasmine's hand with her free one, squeezing it in a way she hoped was reassuring. "They know what they're doing. I have to keep telling myself that."

Jasmine sounded like she was near tears. "They know what they're doing and they're coming back to us."

Pauline knew the technology now existed to produce a perfect clone of a previous iteration, and yet she couldn't bear the thought of losing Aiden again. She wouldn't wish that grief on anyone. "Yes." Her reply sounded more sure than she felt. "They will."

CHAPTER TWENTY-TWO

IT WAS strange to see New Eden from a bird's-eye view. Through the visualizer mounted on the pod's underside, Aiden watched the settlement zip by, the combination of old and new buildings, the fields that were finally thriving. The agri-center would be filled with livestock waiting to be sedated and moved aboard a ship, should the situation come to that.

It won't. Aiden took a deep breath to reassure himself as his pod grew closer to the western side of the settlement. The ocean came into view, the water deceptively calm in the growing darkness. An image of the bomb came to mind, fed to him by the pod, along with a warning that it would detonate within the next thirty minutes.

Thirty minutes? They had a couple of hours the last time they'd checked it. "Goddamn it," he said aloud.

Darius's voice crackled over a speaker. "What is it?"

"Did you get that warning about the bomb?"

The alarm in Darius's voice was palpable. "What fucking warning?"

"We have thirty minutes or less to extract it."

"Fuck!"

Korjek's voice joined them. "You have taken heed of the increased detonation schedule?"

"Yeah," Aiden replied tersely. "It looks like it's not going to go off according to schedule. I'm going under the water now. Can one of you send a warning to the ships? They might have to evacuate earlier."

Darius's voice was just as tense. "On it."

Aiden thought about the cows and chickens in the agricenter, unaware of what was happening around them. He didn't consider himself a sentimental man, but he felt sorry for the poor creatures if they had to die in a tsunami. Hell, he felt sorry for the whole planet.

Pauline. He had to get a message to Pauline. Opening his mind to the pod's controls, he searched for a way to connect with the cyborgs' ship and came up blank. Goddamn it again.

The ship plunged into the water with an undignified crash, taking a few seconds to orient itself. The coordinates Aiden had plugged into the pod had it gliding of its own volition into the sea, the increased pressure making his ears hurt. It took a few seconds for them to return to normal, for his cybernetics to register the change. The pod's exterior lights flashed on, casting a sickly yellow glow through the water, highlighting the silty seafloor's shifting as the pod sped along it. Aiden's unease grew as he got closer to the bomb site. Thirty minutes until detonation, maybe less.

A robotic voice broke through the underwater silence, making him jump in his seat. "Unn flar poch," it announced, then continued babbling in a rapid-fire tongue. The language registered as unknown to Aiden.

"Translate to Standard," he barked.

The voice halted. A whirring noise sounded for half a

second, then the voice said, "The subject's accelerant is breaking down."

"Tell me something I don't know," Aiden snapped.

"The failure of the accelerant will cause an explosion."

"What did I just say?"

"The accelerant will combust when fully exposed to fresh water."

Was talking back to the comp causing its responses? Aiden gritted his teeth and didn't reply. Instead, he moved forward a little, nearly pressing his face against the forward viewport as the pod's incline slowed, his night vision activating. He recognized his surroundings from his first trip underwater. Any second now, the bomb would come into view.

"How are you doing?" Darius asked.

An image of Darius's pod appeared in his mind. It hovered directly above his over the water. Korjek's was under it, about one hundred meters behind him. "I can see it," Aiden reported. The innocuous-looking metal box was exactly where it should be, wedged between two plates. Aiden concentrated, directing the pod's tractor beam to it. The bomb offered some resistance to being eased out of its spot, and the beam gently sawed away at the surrounding plates to pull it out. He felt it being removed, as acutely as if a tooth had been pulled. But it didn't explode.

"Got it," he reported.

"Very good," said Korjek, their voice sounding as close to pleased as Aiden had ever heard it.

The pod's comp spoke again. "Explosive successfully extracted. Accelerant is breaking down."

"Yeah, I know," Aiden muttered. He directed the pod to ascend. "Darius, Korjek, I'm coming up now."

"We'll be waiting," Darius promised.

The pod effortlessly glided through the water, picking

up speed the closer it got to the surface. It broke through with a jolt, the motion making Aiden's teeth rattle, before it shot through the air to its pre-programmed off-world coordinates. The speed made him a little nervous. He'd never moved that quickly before.

"Korjek, is this normal?" he barked into the speaker.

No answer.

His palms grew slick with sweat. "Korjek? Darius? Can either of you hear me?"

The pod's ascent was getting uncomfortable for him. His body fought the pull of gravity. It was going much too fast, a dangerous speed.

"Detonation imminent," the pod's comp said, a touch too cheerfully for Aiden's liking.

"Fuck!" He barely resisted the urge to slam his fists against the command console in frustration.

Some fighter pilot he was. He could hardly control a modified escape pod as it hurtled through the night sky, closer to the New Eden atmosphere. The craft halted for a heart-stopping second, then jostled from side to side as it fought gravity harder than his body was, with him now plastered against the back of the seat.

A clarity seized him, along with the memory of his previous iteration as he crawled through the tunnel aboard the ship, about to be electrocuted. He was going to die again. But he would save New Eden while he did so.

At least I told Pauline I love her before I go.

The pod was launched forward, sending him head-first into the console.

What the fuck?

It took another half second for him to realize that he had done it. The familiar blackness of space surrounded him, the pod suspended in a giant dark vacuum.

"Explosive shell is failing. Detonation will occur in ninety seconds," the pod's comp said.

He'd done it! He'd hauled the bomb off-world! Quickly, Aiden released the tractor beam and directed the pod closer to the planet, away from it. Through the visualizers, he watched as the box drifted away from the pod.

A moment later, the pod was hit with a shockwave so strong, it turned on its side. Aiden's head slammed against the portside viewport, sending stars across his vision. The pod automatically righted itself, the quick shift making his stomach turn over.

His breath caught. Conducting a quick analysis of himself and the pod, he found that both were fully operational. The pod's exterior sensors registered the explosion, the effect tempered by the lack of oxygen but deadly to anything that hadn't been as heavily armored as his pod.

"I did it," he whispered. The tension he'd been carrying in his shoulders relaxed, muscles loosening as the realization of what he'd done set in. Tapping the command console's comms unit, he said, "Mission accomplished. The bomb's gone."

His only response was static.

"For fuck's sake," he groused. He plugged in a course for the empty field where the cyborgs' starship rested, and to his relief, the ship's navigation responded to his command. A damage report popped into his head, noting that the pod's exterior armor should be repaired as soon as possible. Before Aiden could curse again, the report confirmed that the vessel could withstand one more trip breaking planetary atmosphere before the risk to occupants increased. At least Aiden wouldn't burn to a crisp on his descent.

The engine was a little fritzed after its rapid travel, but he could work with that. Settling back against his seat,

Aiden prepared for a slow trip back to New Eden, back to Pauline.

I can hardly wait to see her again.

———

RHYS'S FACE was ashen when he walked into the lounge. Hannah and Jasmine trailed behind him, wearing matching expressions of shock.

Pauline's stomach turned over. For a moment, she thought she might be sick on the deck. She spoke before any of them could. "What happened?"

Rhys looked around the lounge, at the worried faces surrounding him. "The bomb has been safely defused," he announced, but there was a warble to his voice that had Pauline's senses on higher alert. The threat had been averted, but something had gone wrong.

Her next words came out in a low hiss, barely audible over the relieved exclamations from the other New Edeners. "What happened?"

"Pauline, could we speak to you for a minute?" There was a beseeching note in Hannah's voice, like she was afraid Pauline would tear her head off. Pauline supposed that wasn't an entirely irrational fear, given how she had been the last few months.

I will not react that way today. She would speak to Hannah like a mature adult, hear what she had to say, then have a breakdown in private if the situation warranted that. She would *not* make a spectacle of herself. Nodding, she followed them out of the lounge, through the corridor to the ship's bridge.

"Tell me." The words came out flat, a direct order. "He's dead, isn't he?"

Her earlier conviction to remain calm evaporated,

replaced with a familiar, bone-deep sense of terror that left a sour taste in her mouth, her exact reaction when she found out Aiden had died. *And now he's died again.* The knowledge of the improved cloning technology was of little comfort to her as she slid bonelessly into the nearest seat, its leathery covering cool against her skin through the thin fabric of her tunic. Tears welled her eyes, and it took everything she had to keep from wordlessly screaming her rage through the ship, to force everyone else to share in her grief. Her vision swam. Bending over, she put her head between her knees, something she remembered her mother telling her years ago would help prevent fainting. but she had never tried until now.

Rhys's voice was firm. "We don't know that yet."

It took a few seconds for it to register. Raising her head, she caught his eye, then Hannah's and Jasmine's. "What?"

"His pod malfunctioned and broke atmosphere faster than was originally anticipated. Simon and Tibbot are working at the comms tower and got in touch with Korjek and Darius after Aiden left the planet," Jasmine explained. "The comms tower registered an explosion outside the atmosphere."

Pauline's heart gave a painful squeeze before she considered Jasmine's words. "Just one explosion," she said as understanding dawned. "If something went wrong with Aiden's pod, wouldn't there have been two?"

Jasmine nodded, then glanced at Rhys and Hannah, who did the same. "I'm a little more optimistic than they are," she said.

"I don't want false hope," Pauline retorted.

"And I don't think we're offering that to you. Cautious hope, perhaps. Right now, the comms tower is trying to get a hold of Aiden. There was something about the Si'laar tech and what we have in the comms tower that isn't fully compatible, I don't know for sure," Rhys said.

Pauline shot to her feet. "He could be coming back to New Eden now!" She bolted for the bridge's doorway, only stopping when Hannah grabbed her arm.

"We don't know yet," Hannah said gravely.

Pauline shook her off, barely resisting the urge to tell her that she didn't have the right to tell her not to have any hope. She silently reminded herself that Hannah had once waited in this bridge for Rhys to come out of emergency surgery, that she understood how awful it was to wait for someone else to deliver news. "I know," Pauline replied. "I just—I have to go to the comms tower. I think I have to move, you know?" She realized as she said the words that they were the truth. She needed to run, to physically work off some of the tension she'd been holding for hours.

"I get it," Jasmine said, surprising her. "I'm going with you."

Hannah tilted her head, regarding them with a surprised expression on her face.

"I want to see Darius," Jasmine explained. "I need to see both of my guys. I've been waiting around here because I didn't want to get in the way, but..." She glanced at Pauline.

"You know that Darius is all right," she said.

"Yeah."

Pauline forced a smile to her face. "It's okay. You being happy about something good isn't bad. It doesn't mean you don't deserve it." Some of the resentment she had been holding for months seemed to lift—Jasmine's happiness with her partners, Rodelle's new relationship, even Hannah's pregnancy. Their happiness and milestones in life didn't take away opportunities for her.

And she believed, deep in her bones, that Aiden was

still alive, that he wasn't about to have his DNA fed into a cloning tank to reproduce again.

I have to meet him when he lands!

"I have to go," she said hurriedly. Without waiting for a response, she dashed out of the bridge, through the corridors to the open exterior door into the night. The heat had lessened, the cool air a balm as she raced through the settlement to the comms tower. Its lights shone brightly in the darkness, a beacon of hope.

Aiden's a fighter pilot. He knows how to navigate a stupid little escape pod!

She had nearly reached the tower when the sound of something tearing through the sky had her looking up. It reminded her of fabric being ripped in two, albeit much louder. Sparks rained down to the field beside the launch pad where the Si'laar ship still waited, the embers thankfully dying as they hit the grass.

"Aiden," breathed Pauline, watching with horrified fascination as a dark shape fell, then landed with a hard thud on the ground, cutting a short swath through the grass.

Before she could reconsider the wisdom of running to something that might burst into flames at any second, she ran for the pod.

The scent of smoke filled her nostrils as she approached it, her blurry reflection visible in the darkened viewports, courtesy of the twin moons. Before she could look for a rock or something to break into it, one panel opened with a hydraulic hiss. Aiden stumbled out of it, bruises darkening on his face, but otherwise whole. Alive, and in one piece. He blinked when he saw Pauline standing in front of it. "I did it," he announced by way of greeting.

She'd all but forgotten the bomb. As she launched

herself into his arms, he took a step back to balance himself against the pod. He kissed her with the desperation of a man who had been dying of thirst in the desert, then finally reached an oasis. A man who knew he was going to live. His tears mingled with hers, and he didn't let her go for what felt like hours.

When he did, his dark eyes staring into hers, she said, "We were worried."

"You do remember what I promised you?"

"That you would come back in one piece?" She squeezed him tighter. "I remember."

"Then, why were you worried?"

"There was a fucking bomb in space, Aiden!" She heard people behind them and kept her voice low, needing privacy for a few more moments. "I was still terrified of losing you again. I don't think I can handle that."

"Then, it's a good thing I plan on staying on the ground for the foreseeable future." His hands gripped her hips, holding her closer. His voice dropped a couple of decibels, breath ruffling her hair as he whispered in her ear. "You were all I could think about when I was up there. I had to get back to you. I love you, Pauline."

A broken sob escaped her. "I love you too."

He pressed a kiss to her forehead. "Let's go home."

FOUR WEEKS later

Aiden wasn't sure what to expect from a Si'laar ritual. Ollie had organized a party for the naming of Tibbot's baby, working with Korjek to arrange something that melded New Eden and Si'laar cultures for the first infant born in decades in the settlement. At Tibbot's insistence, the naming ceremony would be held on dry land, which Aiden knew had been met with some resistance from their fellow Si'laar. He stayed out of it, as did the other New Edeners, except Ollie. The older man was the only humanoid Korjek consistently listened to.

With Brandon's and Rodelle's help, Aiden and Pauline had baked trays of doughnuts and a sweet confection Brandon called blondies. The couple had all but turned their newly built house into an old-world restaurant, regularly hosting dinners where they showed off their culinary experiments. Brandon had always had a flair for cooking and a healthy disdain for all things remotely military, thanks to his original's being a civilian.

The naming ritual was to be held in the amphitheater,

the only place with enough seating for everyone. When Aiden and Pauline arrived with a bottle of dandelion wine to share, they found most of New Eden already there, enhanced and unenhanced alike. The Si'laar were clustered around a small plastiglas tank in front of the stage, filled with seawater. All of them wore shiny green robes that glowed in the moonlight overhead, the material reminding Aiden of their scaled skin. All of them had arranged their white hair into plaits down their backs. Tibbot held their baby with all four arms, the infant wearing a tiny gold robe. The baby stared at everyone assembled with wide eyes, the pupils silver. Spotting Ollie, who wore a green-dyed tunic and shorts for the occasion, the baby's face stretched into a wide smile and they waved two arms at him.

Connor and James took seats next to Aiden and Pauline. "They're making Ollie the baby's honorary grandfather," James explained by way of greeting. "He's really excited about it."

"I didn't think the Si'laar had that kind of relationship in their culture," Pauline said.

"They don't. Ollie said that they wanted to include him because he and Korjek are so close. I think it's sweet," James replied.

"Maybe Ollie will teach the baby how to play poker. He's a hell of a player," Connor added. He attended Ollie's twice-weekly card games at his house, along with a couple of other cyborgs and Si'laar.

"It's a little early for the kid to be a card shark," muttered James.

Connor gave a noncommittal shrug. "They'll soon have Hannah and Rhys's son to trounce at cards." That bit of news had been very surprising to New Eden, and a sign of further hope for the settlement.

Pauline gave Aiden a knowing smile that made his heart give a happy little flutter. He squeezed her hand in response. They had yet to speak to Connor for confirmation, but both were certain they would have their own baby in a few months. Aiden's sensors had detected an embryo a couple of days before. The idea of parenthood was both exhilarating and terrifying. He could hardly wait for it.

Ollie held up his hands for silence. "Thank you for coming out tonight," he said, beaming at the Si'laar. "This is a very important event for everyone. It is a celebration of the first baby born on New Eden in a very long time, and I'm happy to be part of their naming ritual, and Tibbot is happy that they're going to be brought up somewhere safe. This is, uh—this is pretty straightforward." He glanced at Korjek, who nodded. What they were nodding about, Aiden couldn't tell. "We wear green to acknowledge new life in their unit and because the baby's scales will change from green to gold in the next few weeks, so we're acknowledging the baby is growing up. They'll sing, and the primary parent—Tibbot—drops a ball called a 'nulo' into the water." To Korjek, he asked, "Did I get that right?"

Korjek nodded.

"Good. Then they read the baby's name in the water, and we all get to hold them for a minute. The whole family."

"This is usually conducted in the water," Tibbot explained, shifting the baby to their other side. "But new places to call home mean new rituals."

Ollie stepped aside, and the assembled Si'laar, six in all, began to chant in their language. Their voices joined in a high-pitched falsetto medley, tugging at Aiden's memory. A hazy recollection of an old-world musical entertainment surfaced. Opera, he recalled. One of his previous iterations or his original had sat through an opera or a recording of it, he wasn't sure. It wasn't unpleasant, either way. He hadn't known the Si'laar possessed musical abilities.

Their song lasted seven minutes, after which Tibbot passed the baby to Ollie. They withdrew a small red ball from a pocket of their robe and dropped it into the plastiglas tank. Staring into the water, they waited wordlessly.

The entire amphitheater was silent, fascinated at the ritual before them. Dimly, Aiden heard the lowing of a cow at the agri-center.

"Piklo Edis," Tibbot announced. Raising their head, they gave a brilliant smile to the crowd.

Aiden couldn't help but match Tibbot's grin. Pauline was doing the same, her free hand curled around her belly, still flat. Beside him, James also wore a wide smile, and even the usually stoic Connor looked delighted. A few cheers sounded from around the amphitheater.

Ollie cuddled the baby to his chest for a moment before passing them to Korjek, who pressed their fingertips against the baby's forehead for a few seconds. They murmured something in their language before handing Piklo over to the other Si'laar, who repeated the same touch as Korjek. Tibbot was last, and they pressed a kiss to the top of the baby's head in a very human-like gesture. "Piklo," they said happily, then held them up for everyone to see.

They were met with a resounding cheer and clapping, New Edeners offering congratulations to the Si'laar. A few of them moved forward, and Tibbot held out Piklo to be held and marveled over. The baby smiled and squeaked, waving their tiny hands at their adoring audience.

When Piklo had been returned to Tibbot, attention turned to the pair of tables laden with food. Aiden and Pauline waited at the back of the crowd, watching the happiness play out on the faces of their friends.

A sense of peace had fallen over the settlement in recent days as the realization that it was safe, that it was finally going to thrive. All the older buildings had been replaced since the bomb's extraction, and a couple of Diloran families from Waystation 8305-C, the closest one to New Eden, were planning to move to New Eden in the coming months, interested in living planetside for a spell.

"Should we get some snacks before everything's demolished? I'm starving," Pauline said.

It was in the amphitheater that his previous iteration had seen her for the first time. He remembered it as clearly as if he had been the one to do it. She'd been standing almost in the exact spot she stood now, hungrily looking at the tables. He had seen her through the crowd, and something in him irrevocably changed as he fell in love at first sight.

"This is where it started," he said. "Where I saw you for the first time."

Pauline's eyes widened a little at the memory. "I think it is. I was at that bench." She pointed to one a few meters away.

"That was one of the best nights of my life."

She blushed, probably remembering how quickly they got acquainted with each other. "It was mine too."

"I'm glad we're doing this together," he said quietly. "I'm glad we got to be here tonight for Piklo's ritual. I like that it was held here, where it started for us and New Eden."

Pauline leaned into him, draping an arm around his waist. "I love you."

Aiden pressed a kiss to the top of her head and inhaled, the scent of her soap and skin a comfort. "I love you too. I always have."

Jessica Marting is a sci-fi and paranormal romance author, art enthusiast (not quite an artist, despite all that time in art school), an avid reader, and makeup collector. She lives in Toronto.

Sign up for her newsletter at jessicamarting.com/newsletter for pre-order alerts, sales, freebies, and more.

ALSO BY JESSICA MARTING

Magic & Mechanicals

Wolf's Lady

Sea Change

Bound in Blood

Dragon's Keep

Spellbound

Afterlife

The Searchers

Blood Ties

Blood Moon

Blood Virtue

The Commons

Supernova

Celestial Chaos

Zone Cyborgs

Haven

Paradise

Oasis

Safe Harbor

Sanctuary

Refuge

New Eden

Contact

Bonded

Recharge

Echo

Standalone Novels & Novellas

Spindle's End

Trade Secrets

Neon Vice

Dead Ringer

Rapture

Escape From Europa 10

Castaways

Demon's Favor

Her Purrfect Match